Nov...
Har...
rom...
by Anne Mather
comes to life
on the movie screen

starring
KEIR DULLEA · SUSAN PENHALIGON

Leopard in the Snow

Guest Stars
KENNETH MORE · BILLIE WHITELAW

featuring GORDON THOMSON as MICHAEL
and JEREMY KEMP as BOLT

Produced by JOHN QUESTED and CHRIS HARROP
Screenplay by ANNE MATHER and JILL HYEM
Directed by GERRY O'HARA

An Anglo-Canadian Co-Production

OTHER
Harlequin Romances
by JEAN S. MacLEOD

Island
Stranger

by

JEAN S. MacLEOD

Harlequin Books

TORONTO • LONDON • NEW YORK • AMSTERDAM • SYDNEY

Original hardcover edition published in 1977
by Mills & Boon Limited

ISBN 0-373-02142-9

Harlequin edition published February 1978

PRINTED IN U.S.A.

CHAPTER ONE

THE man stood at the edge of the Bluff gazing down over
Frenchman's Cove at the little group sitting on the coral sand.
Taller than average, his taut jaw hard to the point of ruthlessness, his eagle gaze surveying the scene before him with
calculating intensity, he looked a man used to command,
autocratic in his dealings when the occasion demanded a firm
hand, but fair in all things. The steel-grey eyes searching the
beach with its slanting coconut palms trembling in the morning breeze took in all the land between South Point and Pelican Head, the rich land surrounding Succoth which had
remained neglected for fifteen years. The signs of poor
husbandry were clear to be seen, yet there was a certain
charm about the dilapidated old house nestling behind its
sheltering screen of palms with the low, rugged spur of hills
rising behind it to shield it from the east wind and the incredible blue of the Caribbean Sea stretching before it to the
western horizon with only one small island between.

For several minutes the intruder stood there immovable,
his eyes narrowing as he scanned the rough land sloping
away from the craggy Bluff to the scrub-covered area which
ended abruptly at Morgan's Reach. It was all good land
which had been allowed to run to seed and he turned away
from it impatiently, looking back across the Cove to the
huddled figures basking idly in the sun. Only one of them
faced towards him, and she seemed to be so intent on what
was being said by the others that she apparently did not notice
him. The other three had their backs to his rugged vantage-
point, oblivious to the fact that they were being watched. In
their scant bathing gear they looked like a conclave of
Indians, he thought dismissively as he turned abruptly to

5

walk back across the Bluff, but no doubt they were part of Succoth and, therefore, interesting.

Before he passed completely out of sight he paused once more, gazing out towards the Atlantic with a ruthlessness about his jaw that suggested a firmness of purpose which would not be denied.

The four young people sitting down in Frenchman's Cove had formed a tight circle, hugging their bare knees as they dug their toes into the warm, silver sand, but suddenly one of them—the boy—lay back, shading his eyes with his hands.

'It's an odd situation,' he observed, 'but one we can't do very much about. After all, we more or less expected to be turned out once the island changed hands.' His blue eyes sought the bluer horizon's rim where a three-masted schooner sailed lazily, blown by the warm trade wind on its journey to one of the islands. 'Of course all this is idyllic, but we didn't expect to go on living on Millo for ever.'

'You didn't,' his elder sister agreed, turning on her side to look at him, 'and I'm resigned to the idea now, but what about Jacinthe and Makeda?'

She looked across at her younger sister who sat next to Jacinthe, who was their cousin, aware of the tension in their faces as they listened.

'Makeda,' she persisted, 'what are you going to do?'

The girl on the other side of the circle seemed to shake herself free from some impossible dream as she unclasped her knees and leaned back on her hands. She could feel the warmth of the sun on the sand and the caress of the gentle wind on her golden skin, and she lifted her face to it for a moment before she answered her sister's question.

'I don't know, Abi. Perhaps I haven't any real choice.' Her mouth grew rebellious and her eyes were suddenly dark with resentment. 'I never thought we would have to leave the island; I imagined we were on Millo for the rest of our lives. Oh,' she added when her sister would have rejected the idea out of hand, 'I don't mean you. I know you're dedicated to your nursing, and I envy you because you've got what you wanted. Going back to New York is your idea of complete fulfilment, though you must feel sad about Millo, too. You won't be able to come here much longer to lie in the sun and go back "renewed". You've said that often enough:'

'There are other islands,' Abi answered philosophically, shaking back her long auburn hair. 'Other places in the sun.'

'Such as Virginia Beach or Miami!' her brother suggested with a mocking smile. 'Or even the Bahamas.'

'The Bahamas are nearer to New York,' Abi pointed out. 'It will all depend on where Mother decides to settle.'

'She won't make a final choice just yet.' There was a degree of hope in Makeda's voice as she uttered the swift prediction. 'She said so the other day. She'll wait till you graduate, Heber.'

Her brother turned over on to his chest, scrutinising the tiny grains of coral sand as he ran them through his strong brown fingers.

'That will take another year—maybe two, if I fail to pass first go,' he frowned. 'Then—who knows? I may decide to go to England, since it was where we were born.'

Eagerly Makeda turned towards him.

'Does that mean you hope to follow in Father's footsteps?' she asked. 'Heber, it's a wonderful idea, and he would have been so proud if he had known. But perhaps you told him before he went away on that last fatal dig?' she added. 'Before he left Millo for the last time.'

Heber shook his head.

'No, I didn't,' he confessed. 'Maybe it was—afterwards that I gave it my undivided attention.' He got to his feet, stretching his thin body in the sun. 'But aren't we jumping the gun a bit? I have another year to do before I'm a qualified geologist and a good many things can happen in a year.' He looked down at Makeda. 'You're the only one who'll be immediately involved,' he pointed out, 'if you mean to go on with the research you were doing for him.'

'I intend to finish his book.' A determined look came into Makeda's eyes, making her appear older. 'It meant more than anything else to him, in the end,' she added, 'and we were half-way through the first set of notes when he left for

Cairo. I've carried on since then as best I could, but I can't do any more till we've heard from the London solicitors. If there are no more notes among his personal effects,' she added unsteadily, 'then my usefulness will be at an end, but I feel that there must be another batch of them on their way here, enough to complete the MS and send it off to the publishers.'

Her father, an eminent archaeologist, and his colleague, Professor George Hunt, had disappeared six months previously on a journey from Egypt to Saudi Arabia, where they had hoped to find further evidence in support of their theory that King Solomon's Mines of Ophir had not been the only source of riches to be found beneath the desert sands. The copious notes which Makeda had been sorting and finally typing for him had made her heart pound with excitement, and she had been glad of her comparative isolation on their Caribbean island while she applied herself to her lengthy task. Of his three children, she had been the only one who had been content to stay on Millo, dedicated to his memory as she worked on his book, knowing that it had been his great ambition to set the facts of many years of diligent research and endeavour before an interested public. She had come to consider herself his chief assistant, as far as the book was concerned, and she had known herself greatly beloved. All the warm affection of which she was capable had been given to the quiet man who had brought her up to appreciate the beauty of the world and recognise the wonders of the past, and she had been greatly shattered by his untimely death.

Of course, they had all been shocked in their separate ways when the news had been relayed to them from London—Abi, and Heber, and Jacinthe, and her mother, least of all perhaps, because Dolly Garland had never really understood the man she had married in London twenty-five years ago. Their interests had been poles apart, and even on Millo they had known the restlessness of divided affections. After the birth of her son, Dolly had had little time for anything else, and latterly she had spent much of the year in England, intent upon his education, leaving her daughters in the care of her husband, who had leased Millo fourteen years ago in the hope of providing his family with an established home.

Dolly had rejected Millo almost immediately, although she found it a convenient refuge from England during the winter months. Mammy and Ben had more or less taken her place in her daughters' affection and Jacinthe had joined them on Millo during the school holidays, a small, frail orphan when her parents had been drowned in a boating accident off Jamaica. With no one else to turn to in such a dire emergency Jacinthe had come to consider herself part of the Professor's family, helping out in the house when she had finally left school and seemingly without any other ambition than to stay on Millo for the rest of her life.

Both Makeda and Jacinthe were true children of the Islands, loving their home, however dilapidated it might have grown over the years, and Jacinthe seemed to be paying scant attention to the argument on hand. A quiet, introspective girl, she looked much younger than her seventeen years, her fair hair, which she had dried in the sun, held back from her thin, oval face by two elastic bands, her body scarcely developed and burned as brown as a Carib's. They had been swimming all morning, each with the distressing knowledge in her heart that their absolute freedom might be ruthlessly curtailed by the dire change of circumstance which neither of them had expected.

Makeda looked across the circle at her silent cousin whose gaze was fixed on the higher ground on the far side of the Cove.

'What's the matter?' she asked. 'You look surprised.'

'Someone has been standing on the Bluff watching us,' Jacinthe said, speaking for the first time.

They turned with one accord to look across the narrow stretch of water between the sands and the spur of rock which ran down into the sea on the northern side of the Cove.

'There's nobody there,' Abi pointed out unnecessarily. 'You must have been dreaming.'

Jacinthe held her breath for a moment.

'I don't dream all that easily.' She found Abi's abrupt materialism disconcerting at times. 'The man was there while you were arguing. I saw him because I was the only one facing that way. He was very tall and he wore a red shirt and blue jeans and stood out quite clearly against the sky.'

'It could have been old Ben or one of the children,' Abi suggested indifferently as she rose to pull on her cotton shift.

'Mammy never allows the children on to the Bluff, it's too dangerous,' Jacinthe pointed out. 'Besides, it was a man. I saw him quite plainly, no matter what you say!'

'Well, he's gone now.' Abi moved her attention to the line of coconut palms slanting across the beach at the southernmost point of the island. 'Anyone ready for a swim?' she asked.

'We've been swimming all morning.' Makeda rose to her feet, digging her toes into the warm sand as she looked back towards the Bluff. 'Someone ought to go up to the house just in case we *have* a visitor.'

'Mammy will cope,' Abi declared. 'Besides, we're not likely to have visitors until the trader comes in tomorrow morning.'

'Unless it was a yacht,' Makeda mused, her brows drawn together in a swift frown.

'They would have come into the Cove. It's the best anchorage,' Heber reminded them as he made ready to follow Abi back into the sea. 'But maybe you'd better check.'

Jacinthe followed Makeda up the beach.

'I wasn't day-dreaming,' she protested. 'Really, I wasn't! The man was there. He walked away across the Bluff in the direction of Green Turtle Bay.'

'I'll go and see,' Makeda volunteered without further ado. 'You go back to the house in case he's gone round the head of the Cove towards Succoth. Mammy might not know what to say to him.'

'I think he was a complete stranger.' Jacinthe stopped in her tracks to look at her cousin, her blue eyes full of a deep concern. 'Supposing it has something to do with Millo changing hands?'

Makeda gave the idea a moment's consideration, her cheeks flushed, her eyes unusually hard.

'Why should the island be involved?' she demanded. 'If this—person had something to do with Millo changing hands we would have heard about it before now. Mr Pettigrew would have written to us from Barbados, or come over with the trader if it was really urgent. Besides, Mother's over there just now and she will probably bring back the latest news.'

'When she comes,' Jacinthe murmured beneath her breath. 'You do know she intends to go to England with Heber?'

'She said she might,' Makeda acknowledged abruptly, 'but Heber may not want her to go. After all, he's nearly twenty-two. She can't go trailing after him for the rest of his life.'

'It's going to be difficult for Heber,' Jacinthe sighed. 'Of course, she's very fond of him.'

'Which isn't exactly an absolute excuse.' Makeda was reminded of her father, baffled and angry by her mother's complete indifference to him. 'I think Heber will tell her so, in the end,' she concluded.

'She'll be terribly hurt,' Jacinthe suggested. 'Don't you want me to come with you to Green Turtle?'

'In case I'm abducted, or something equally terrifying?' Makeda laughed. 'Your "man on the Bluff" must have come by sea, since there's no other way of reaching Millo, but I hardly think he'll be a pirate, as you seem to fear! He's far more likely to be someone off a yacht exploring to stretch his legs before they set sail again, and we've probably seen the last of him—if he was ever there at all!' she teased.

'Makeda! I wouldn't say it if it wasn't so,' her cousin protested. 'I'm not like you, full of imagination and the determination to keep Millo for yourself.'

'It *is* private,' Makeda returned, 'but that's not my only reason for wanting to keep it so. You know I love Millo and —and what I'm going to do without it I can't tell!'

Standing in the deep shade of the coconut palms, she looked very young and completely vulnerable. She was eighteen, one year older than Jacinthe, but the sun on her face and the wind blowing her auburn hair back from her high forehead made her look many years younger. Her slim, bronzed body was encased in an old bathing suit which she had worn since her schooldays, and she had thrust her feet into a pair of battered sandals to walk across the scrub, disdaining the fashionable blue shift which Abi had offered her when she had followed Heber into the sea.

'Go back to Succoth,' she said in a choked whisper, 'and look after Mammy and the children.'

The day had started disastrously, she mused as she climbed towards the Bluff. She had quarrelled with Abi and argued with Heber, all to no account, simply because they had taken this careless attitude towards Millo. Her beloved island really meant nothing to them. It had been a place to come back to in the holidays while they were all at school, a remote shelter which their mother had never liked, and now they were preparing to abandon it with a lightheartedness which she could not understand. All the love and affection of which she was capable had been given to Millo in the past and she could not bear to think of the time when she might have to leave it.

Heber had stressed the point of their likely departure over breakfast, which Mammy had served to them on the verandah, and tears had run unashamedly down the old woman's ebony cheeks. In her big white cooking apron Mammy had looked completely stricken, and Makeda, at least, had understood how she felt. The fact that she was about to be abandoned had reduced Mammy to speechlessness, but the slow tears had told their own particular tale. A life of faithfulness and loyal service could be coming to an abrupt end, and Mammy had nowhere else to go. She and Ben had come to Succoth when John Garland had leased Millo all those years ago and they had expected to stay on the island for the remainder of their lives.

Makeda felt as forlorn as the old Carib servant, although she could not shed any tears. The life she loved was about to be changed, and the hard lump at the back of her throat as she reached the highest point of the Bluff threatened to choke her. She could not look towards the future with any

12

real hope, as Abi and Heber did, because all she had ever wanted was to remain here in Millo, where she belonged.

The unshed tears misted her eyes for a moment when she looked down towards the sloping land which led through a grove of mahogany trees to the sunlit water of Green Turtle Bay. It wasn't exactly a safe anchorage because of the coral reef which almost enclosed it, but if you knew what you were about and had enough experience it was possible to sail into the quiet water of the bay and seek shelter beneath the ruins of Crichton Place. And beneath the promontory where Crichton's stood like a deserted ghost, a beautiful little ketch had put down her anchor.

Makeda had handled boats for as long as she could remember, sailing with her father when he returned to Millo from his searches around the world and then with Heber when they were old enough to go out alone, and her eyes lit up for a moment as she took in the clean lines of the little craft sheltering in the lee of the headland. It had been anchored close inshore, well away from the Albatross Bank, which suggested that the navigator had come to stay for more than just an hour or two while he explored the interior of yet another Caribbean island. The Grenadines were popular with sailing craft and cruisers alike right through the season, and it wasn't the first time that one of them had ventured into Green Turtle Bay, but Makeda had climbed across the Bluff with a deep resentment in her heart, sparked off by her conversation with the others in Frenchman's Cove.

Waiting for several minutes on the sloping ground which led down to the bay so that whoever was on board the ketch would see her and come on deck, she looked up at the grey walls of Crichton Place standing on a slight elevation above her. The house had never been occupied in all the years they had lived on Millo, having fallen into disrepair in the early part of the century when it had become uncommercial to grow sugar-cane on the smaller islands, but once it had been an elegant plantation house with its colonnaded portico and rows of long windows on two floors and a view westward into the sunset.

It was a view she loved because Green Turtle had become her secret bay, the quiet hideaway where she had found refuge when things were going wrong at Succoth. It was a place for dreaming and finding eventual peace, and it had been her undisputed domain all through her childhood because of the absurd belief that Crichton's was haunted. Long ago Heber had explored the uninhabited house and left it at that, but Mammy and Ben and the children wouldn't go near the place. The scrub had grown high around it, but the rows of splendid mahogany trees which the original owner must have planted still marked the position of a driveway winding down from Crichton's to the shore.

Even after she had waited for another five minutes, there was no movement from the ketch. The owner could be asleep in the cabin, of course, lulled by the gentle movement of the water inside the reef, and not likely to appear for some considerable time, but the longer she looked the more convinced she became that the elegant little craft was indeed unoccupied.

Curiosity overcame her, at last. Loving boats and being as much at home on the sea as on shore, she walked down on to the coral sand, kicked off her shabby footwear, and waded out into the warm green water until she could swim. Times without number she had come to Green Turtle Bay to put her world in order, but suddenly it seemed that she had no real right to be here. The conversation of the morning still perturbed her and she approached the anchored ketch with an odd sort of rage in her heart. Why couldn't it all be the same as it had always been on Millo? Why had there to be change and heartache and tears?

She bit her lip on the tears, swimming with hardly a sound round the stern of the anchored ketch, although she knew now with that strange, inexplicable instinct which comes with long contact with seafaring that the little yacht was indeed unoccupied. It had a deserted look, but had not been abandoned. Everything on deck was ship-shape, and when she raised herself up to peer briefly through one of the port-holes the cabin it served was also immaculate. The man who

14

had been standing on the Bluff, according to Jacinthe, was still ashore.

Which meant that he had gone to Succoth and was probably there now being entertained by Jacinthe and even by Mammy, who would be reassured by her cousin's presence.

Turning on to her back, she confessed inwardly that she had come to Green Turtle Bay for that very reason. She had not wanted to meet a stranger at that moment, however fleeting his visit to Millo might be. She had wanted time to be alone, time to adjust to the thought of change, and seeking sanctuary at Green Turtle had become second nature to her. Now that she could swim unmolested in warm water enclosed by its guardian reef she felt secure.

Slowly she paddled across the bay, still on her back with her face upturned to the sky, her hair, darkly wet, floating on the surface. It was long and straight, with a red sheen on it when she dried it in the sun, and she never swam with a cap. It was something she didn't think about, just as she often swam naked when she was alone.

Coming out of the water at the far side of the bay, she peeled off the top part of her bathing suit to let her arms and shoulders dry evenly in the sun, raising her arms above her head with a sudden feeling of wellbeing which was difficult to assess. At least, she was free here, she concluded; at least, she was unobserved.

Before her hair had dried she saw the man at the entrance to Crichton's. He stood beneath the portico which commanded a broad vista to the open sea beyond the reef, and he remained quite still, the bright red shirt he wore making a splash of unexpected colour, like some kind of challenge, against the weathered stone of the deserted house. His tall, sparse figure was framed in the aperture which had once been the door, and even from that distance there was a look of supreme arrogance about him.

Makeda slipped the straps of her bathing suit on to her shoulders, wondering how long he had been standing there, watching. Then, with an angry light in her eyes, she marched straight up the beach to confront the intruder.

They met half way along the overgrown drive and because her feet hurt and it was cooler under the mahogany trees, she scowled at him, hugging her bare arms across her chest.

'Good morning,' he said with a whimsical smile. 'I thought you were a mermaid!'

He had been standing up there at Crichton's longer than she thought, and the knowledge was suddenly confusing.

'What are you doing here?' she demanded. 'You must know you're trespassing.'

His look was suddenly calculating, the smile wiped from his lean face as he met the hard expression in her eyes.

'It's something I hadn't thought about,' he assured her calmly. 'The sea is free to all comers and a safe anchorage is nobody's prerogative.'

'It's like a millpond beyond the reef,' she pointed out without quite knowing why. 'There was absolutely no danger, no reason for you to seek shelter in the bay.'

'I see that most of my danger is on land,' he observed, taking in her scant attire and brown limbs in one amused glance. 'You live here, of course.'

She drew herself up.

'It's my home,' she said. 'My name is Makeda Garland and I've lived here most of my life.'

'Makeda?' he repeated, shortening the distance between them on the overgrown drive.

'It was the name of the Queen of Sheba,' she told him without hesitation. 'My father gave it to me because his work was bound up with that period of history. He was doing research in Saudi Arabia when he died.'

He had been watching her keenly.

'You miss him greatly,' he suggested. 'I believe I can understand how you feel.'

'How could you?' To her horror her voice had caught on a note of anguish. 'You didn't know him, so how could you possibly have any idea of how I feel?'

'It was easy to hazard a guess,' he said in that maddeningly calm voice which succeeded in putting her at a disadvantage. 'Why are you so upset?'

'I——' She stood on the drive before him, not quite knowing what to say to this calm intruder who evidently took her for a child, and an obnoxious one at that.

'Confession is good for the soul,' he reminded her. 'Will you come on board and have something warm to drink? You look chilled to the bone.'

'I don't feel the cold,' she told him defensively. 'I suppose it was coming up under the trees that made me shiver.'

'All the same, Sheba, I think you should allow me to make you a cup of cocoa,' he persisted. 'You're much too young for grog.'

He had said it: he had more or less told her that she was a petulant child ridding herself of a perverse mood by being aggressive over her secret domain.

'I'm eighteen,' she announced with dignity, 'but I don't think I need your "grog" to warm me up. I just wondered who you were, since we noticed you on the Bluff a short while ago. You seemed to be on a tour of inspection, or was it just idle curiosity?'

'Curiosity, I think.' He had not shown the surprise she had expected at the mention of her age. 'But not idle. I never do anything without a motive.'

'In that case, I can't think what reason you must have for inviting me on board your yacht,' she returned.

His smile was decidedly crooked as he looked down the driveway.

'Apart from coming up barefoot over all this rubble, you probably haven't a wrap of any kind,' he surmised. 'A mermaid's life is all very well if you keep in the sea, but it can be a chilly business walking about on land, especially under trees.'

'I was about to swim back across the bay,' she assured him.

He glanced behind them at the averted face of Crichton's.

'I thought you were going up there,' he said. 'You know its history, I suppose?'

'It was the original plantation house,' she explained, walking with him into the sunshine. 'It must have been a beautiful place when it was new and lived in by a happy family.

Can't you imagine their little world—everything here on the island that they really needed and the satisfaction of endeavour? It must have been quite perfect until the curse hit them.'

'The curse?' he repeated, highly amused. 'Surely you don't believe in anything so utterly primitive?'

Makeda bit her lip.

'You asked me about Crichton's and I've told you,' she declared. 'Curse or not, it began to decay over the years and now you can see it as it is. If there had been a male Crichton living there for any length of time it could have survived. It was built to last, as you see, but after two hurricanes when no repairs had been made the main part of the roof caved in. Besides, there was a disastrous fire——'

She hesitated, aware that he was now looking beyond her, thinking, no doubt, how foolish she was to believe in hoodoo and curses, like a primitive Carib.

'The fire was the final catastrophe,' he suggested. 'After that, I suppose they just gave up and moved out, lock, stock and barrel without a fight.'

She knew that she had to defend Crichton's, although she was far too young ever to have known its owner.

'Sarah Crichton was the only one left, in the end. She couldn't cope on her own, but she must have gone reluctantly, leaving all this behind.'

The passionate note of regret did not escape his notice.

'You feel some sort of affinity with her,' he suggested. 'Is it because you may have to leave your own home now that your father is dead?'

She nodded abruptly.

'Was that what this morning's conference was all about?' he asked. 'Over there on the other side of the Bluff?'

Makeda bridled at the personal question.

'It was a purely family affair,' she returned frigidly.

'Point taken!' They had reached the water's edge. 'Satisfy your curiosity in return for mine,' he offered. 'Then we can call it quits. Come aboard.'

'How?' she demanded. 'Did you swim over?'

He shook his head.

'I have a respectable dinghy over there under the palms.'

She could see it now, fastened by its painter to one of the slanting boles and her curiosity about the immaculate little ketch tempted her to accept his invitation.

'Are you handling her alone?' she asked, at which he laughed outright.

'You needn't worry about your virtue, Sheba. Just come!'

'Because you want to know more about Crichton's,' she suggested. 'Well, there isn't a lot more to tell. Sarah Crichton did go away, and she died soon afterwards, in Bermuda.'

'So much for the curse,' he said. 'Why was it wished on the family in the first place?'

'It was a long time ago.' She could not think why she was telling him about the ancient legend since she had never really believed in it. 'The very first Crichton—David, I think his name was—made a lot of money before he ever came to the island. He made it mostly from slave-labour, but when he built Crichton Place he put all that behind him. He was a good master and there was a well-run native village down here on the shore. You can still see the remains of it over there where you've left your dinghy.'

He nodded.

'I wondered about the old foundations,' he said. 'I guessed there must have been a settlement of some kind, although I took it for a derelict fishing port.'

'The Caribs were free to do as they wished in their own time,' Makeda explained. 'They fished and cultivated the land round the shore.'

'Then why curse a benevolent master?' he queried.

'It wasn't David Crichton they cursed, it was his son.'

'Aha! Now we're getting down to the essential facts. Crichton, junior, was another Absalom, I take it?'

'In a way,' she had to agree. 'He was wildly extravagant and his father could do nothing with him. Half his time he was in Trinidad or Jamaica, and when he did come home to Crichton Place it was not to work. He played around, and one day a native girl was found strangled on the beach.'

'And so the curse was laid very firmly on Crichton's by the Indians?'

'Yes. It said that a male heir would never survive his childhood. It's all rather ghastly, but it did turn out that way,' Makeda insisted. 'No male Crichton ever lived long enough to inherit the Place, and eventually the family died out.'

They had reached the dinghy and he stood looking down at it in silence.

'For my money I think a nice, sedate marriage would have cancelled all that out. There's nothing like an uncomplicated relationship between two people for laying ghosts and stamping out legends. Did your father buy the lease from the last of the Crichtons?'

Makeda shook her head.

'Millo changed hands several times after Sarah Crichton died. The subsequent owners were all strangers to the island,' she added, 'and they did nothing about the Place. It remained deserted, as you see it now.'

They ran the dinghy down to the water's edge where he turned back to look at Crichton's, as if the old legend held him in thrall.

'I can hardly expect you to believe in the curse since you don't know the Islands,' Makeda said.

'I couldn't doubt you, Sheba,' he returned lightly. 'The hallmark of truth is on everything you say. How long have you been hiding away in your secret domain?'

'Hiding?' With one bare leg over the dinghy's stern she paused to challenge him. 'What do you mean?'

'You haven't come in contact with the outside world very much,' he suggested.

'I was educated on Barbados and, finally, in England.'

'In some secluded seminary for young ladies, I expect.'

'Is there anything wrong with that?' she asked. 'I'm quite happy the way I am.'

'Obviously.'

She was in two minds now whether to accept his invitation or not, but suddenly her mouth firmed. Why should she care what he thought about her? She was used to being baited about her name, although nobody had done it quite so deliberately before, and she *did* want to see over the ketch. Her love of boats finally won the day.

'Are you going to row?' he asked, pausing before he stepped into the tiny craft.

'Why not?' she said, moving over. 'It's the sort of primitive exercise I do rather well.'

He waded into the shallow water, pushing off as she fitted the oars into the rowlocks.

'How long have you been at Succoth this time?' he asked.

'Two years.' She was faintly surprised that he should know the name of her home. 'I've been working with my father on the notes he made on his first visit to Saudi Arabia. I learned to type at my "secluded seminary for young ladies", you see, and I can spell. My father was writing a book.'

In spite of her efforts to control her emotion her voice had faltered and she looked at him in despair.

'He left the book unfinished, I gather?'

'Yes. When he went off on this final dig I was half-way through the first batch of notes, and now they're finished.'

'Which means you can't complete his book until you have the next consignment, if any?' he queried.

'Something like that.' She considered him warily. 'What do you do for a living?' she demanded.

He thought for a moment.

'I suppose you could say I was a property developer,' he answered, his gaze fixed on the other island which lay just outside the reef.

'It would be no use to you,' she informed him sharply. 'Nobody has ever lived on Pelican Island, although it's almost joined to Millo by the reef. The coral can only be used as a causeway when the tide is out, and even then it can be dangerous. There's a treacherous underwater bank out there—the Albatross—where the tide runs between the islands.'

'I avoided it,' he acknowledged. 'I haven't come to buy Pelican Island, although it did interest me at first. I discovered, finally, that it had no adequate harbour.'

Something cold seemed to touch Makeda's heart.

'You would prefer Millo, of course,' she suggested, 'but it's not for sale.'

'No,' he said, as if he already knew that her beloved island had already changed hands. 'What will you do when you have to leave? Go back to England?'

She caught a nasty crab with one of the oars, utterly disconcerted by his abrupt question.

'I may have to,' she answered truthfully. 'It's all in the melting-pot at present, but I think my mother will go to England with Heber. He's my brother,' she added quickly.

'Ah!' he observed in the maddening way he had. 'It all fits. The other members of your family don't really mind about leaving the island. Only you.'

'And Jacinthe—she's my cousin—but she will do exactly as Mother tells her.'

'What age is Jacinthe?'

'Seventeen. Younger than me.'

'Sheba! No one could be younger than you are,' he smiled. 'You are the eternal innocent.'

She did not consider his remark a compliment.

'I can think for myself,' she declared, 'however young I may look. I want to stay on Millo—of course I do—but when the time comes and I have to go I'll be able to cope with that, too.'

They had reached the ketch and he allowed her to clamber aboard unassisted.

'I dare say you have a boat of your own,' he remarked.

'It's my brother's, really, but I use it most of the time now that he's away at college. I suppose,' she added dolefully, 'it will have to go, too.'

He led the way along the deck without answering.

'I'll make you some cocoa,' he offered when they finally reached the galley. 'There are biscuits in that tin over there.'

It was slightly chilly below decks and she suddenly felt the need for her non-existent wrap.

'If you're cold,' he suggested casually, 'there's a towelling jacket in the after-cabin.'

She went in search of it, finding it on a hook behind the door where he had probably hung it after shaving. It was far too big for her, of course, but she shrugged herself into its protective warmth, folding back the cuffs twice to free her hands. The jacket came down as far as her knees, the thick towelling belt holding it together somewhere about her narrow hips, and she supposed that she looked more childish than ever, huddled up inside it.

Digging her bare toes into the thick pile of the carpet, she looked about her with a natural curiosity. The ketch was a rich man's toy and she had never been on board a luxury yacht before. All her experience had been gained the hard way, sitting out in a narrow, slatted well, but she would not have had it otherwise although she was willing, in all honesty, to grant her new acquaintance the experience since he was sailing the ketch single-handed. The powerful engine in the wheelhouse was rarely used, she suspected, going on deck to find him already waiting there with two mugs by his side.

'Cocoa.' He indicated the nearest mug. 'I've nothing more than a wheaten biscuit to offer you, I'm afraid.'

'That suits me fine,' Makeda assured him, accepting a biscuit from the tin he proffered. 'What are you drinking?'

'Grog,' he informed her with a detached smile. 'The Curse of the Crichtons chilled me to the bone!'

'Since you didn't believe a word of it, you really don't deserve the grog!'

He leaned forward, looking directly into her eyes.

'It's what *you* believe that matters,' he said. 'If Crichton's belonged to you what would you do with it?'

She sipped the cocoa while she considered the hypothetical question.

'I would restore it,' she said, at last, 'if I had the money to spend. I would put a new roof on it and a new door, but I wouldn't touch the stonework because it has mellowed over the years. I'd leave the windows as they are now, narrow and long, so that I could step out into the garden whenever I liked and run down to the beach.'

'In your bare feet,' he added with an amused smile. 'The drive would have to be smoothed off to make it easier for you.' Suddenly he bent and rubbed the back of his fingers across her cheek. 'Sheba, you have a wonderful imagination,' he said. 'One day you may see Crichton's like that.'

Makeda drew back from his touch. It had been soft and impersonal, a gesture of amused tolerance, no doubt, but it had left her with an odd feeling of vulnerability, shaking her inwardly for no very clear reason except that it had been so utterly unexpected. He wasn't the sort of man who would indulge in a light flirtation on the shortest possible acquaintance, she thought. Or was he?

Looking into his dark face, she came to the conclusion, once again, that he was treating her as a child.

She laid her mug down on the deck.

'I'm quite warm now,' she said. 'Thank you for the cocoa.' She began to untie the belt of the towelling jacket. 'Thank you for this, too. I won't need it any more.'

He rose as she stood poised on the side of the ketch, ready to dive.

'I ought to tell you my name,' he said.

'I don't think it matters very much.' Her hands were stretched out above the water. 'We're not likely to meet again.'

'You never know,' he said. 'I may even think of acquiring Pelican Island, after all.'

'To add to your empire?' She turned to look at him, her voice vibrating with anger. 'You shouldn't think twice about building an ugly big holiday hotel right on the foreshore, would you? A Caribbean Hilton or something equally unpleasant.'

'I only offered to tell you my name!' he protested.

'I don't think I want to know,' she returned briskly. 'Quite possibly I won't be on Millo by the time you come to Pelican —if you really mean to turn it into a second Antigua.'

'Antigua is still very beautiful, even though it's a popular holiday playground nowadays.'

'It's changed, just like all the other islands,' she declared sensitively. 'Most of its charm has gone.'

'But not all. You can't rub out several centuries of history just by building a few hotels.' His jaw was hardened, although there was still a gleam of amusement in his eyes. 'When you're mad, Makeda, you look magnificent! The name is Ogilvie, by the way—Grant Ogilvie, in case we do stumble upon each other somewhere in the future.'

The splash of her dive drowned out any laughter which may have pursued her on her way to the shore.

Picking up her beach shoes on the far side of the bay, she glanced back at the ketch, but there was no sign of Grant Ogilvie on deck and it looked as deserted as when she had first seen it.

Hastily she made her way over the Bluff to arrive at Succoth as the others were gathering on the verandah for a belated lunch. Mammy had set a huge wooden bowl of fruit on the wicker table outside the dining-room where the jalousies were closed against the heat of the sun, and Abi had cut herself a piece of pineapple to eat with the figs and grated coconut already on her plate. Jacinthe sat at the far end of the table, gazing down at a paw-paw as if she had very little appetite even for the fruit, but Heber's plate was piled high with a more substantial selection of sweet potatoes and eddoes to complement the flying fish he had brought up from the beach.

'I don't know how you can eat them,' Makeda chided as she passed his chair. 'You're a complete Philistine! They're so delicate and beautiful.'

'You're talking about the flying fish?' He looked up to query her statement. 'But there are millions of them,' he protested. 'They practically give themselves up. In fact, they'll commit suicide on your deck if you wait long enough.'

Makeda selected a ripe avocado pear.

'This will do for me,' she said. 'I'm not very hungry.'

'Where yo' bin, Miss Makeda?' Mammy came to the doorway to ask. 'I got some nice crane chub fo' dinner if yo' was invitin' yo' young man to eat with yo'.'

Makeda frowned.

25

'My "young man"? Now, who might that be, Mammy?'

'Ben say he see yo' over at Green Turtle with a nice young man on a white yacht.' Mammy's smile split her black face almost from ear to ear. 'Yo' know ol' Ben he never makes a mistake. He has good eyesight, that ol' man!'

Abi turned in her chair.

'Not Jacinthe's "man in the red shirt"!' she exclaimed. 'So that's why you stayed away so long! Confess everything!' She scooped a spoonful of coconut into her mouth.

Makeda flushed scarlet.

'There's absolutely nothing to confess,' she declared. 'I *did* meet "Jacinthe's man", as you call him, but he's not important. He came into Green Turtle to explore, I suppose, and he didn't tell me anything about himself, except——'

'Except?' Heber prompted between two mouthfuls of sweet potatoes.

'He said he was a property developer.'

Abi sat bolt upright.

'Do you suppose he wants to develop Millo?' she asked. 'That would be fun!'

'Not for Makeda. She wants to keep Millo as it is for ever, a virgin island dedicated to her own desire!' Heber emptied his plate. 'How did you get on to his yacht?'

Jacinthe was listening intently now.

'I swam out to take a closer look at it,' Makeda confessed.

'The devil, you did!' her brother laughed. 'And I suppose your property developer hauled you aboard and threatened to make off with you all the way round to Morgan's Reach!'

'Don't be ridiculous!' Makeda bit into the avocado pear. 'He came down from Crichton's, as a matter of fact—quite unexpectedly.'

Heber eyed her scanty bathing attire.

'Were you dressed like that or entirely in the nude?' he enquired.

Makeda turned her back on him.

'I refuse to answer any more silly questions,' she said. 'I told you he wasn't at all important.'

26

'And there the matter ought to rest! Has he gone?' Heber asked.

'I don't know, but I shouldn't think he would be there in the morning.'

'Hard luck!' Her brother scraped back his chair. 'What was he doing at Crichton's? Just looking?'

'Why not? He must have noticed it from the sea.'

'I wonder why he didn't moor in the Cove,' Abi said. 'It's a much better anchorage than Green Turtle with all that coral around.'

'Perhaps he saw Succoth and decided not to land right on our doorstep,' Makeda suggested.

'He did come over the Bluff,' Jacinthe pointed out, 'as if he knew we were here. What was he like, Makeda?'

'You were first to see him.' Makeda knew that she was evading the issue because she felt that she could not adequately describe the stranger. 'He's tall and dark and given to sarcasm, and he took me for a ten-year-old.'

Abi laughed.

'And I'm sure you told him you were at least twenty!'

'I told him the truth. Probably I *do* look years younger than the sophisticated women he's used to meeting,' Makeda allowed.

'Ah, well!' Abi rose to her feet. 'That's that, I suppose, since you *didn't* ask him to dinner.'

'I didn't even think about it,' Makeda returned, 'since we weren't exactly on those sort of terms.'

'Yet you went on board his yacht?'

'I was—curious about it,' Makeda confessed. 'In fact, I swam out to take a closer look.'

'And he caught you in the act!' Abi was vastly amused. 'You *were* wearing your bathing suit?'

'Of course I was!' A wave of embarrassment sent a dark colour into Makeda's cheeks. 'I met him coming down from Crichton Place.'

'Do you think he really was just a snooper?' Jacinthe asked more seriously.

'We've had them on the island before,' Makeda reminded her. 'Why should Grant Ogilvie be any different?'

'Grant Ogilvie?' Abi repeated. 'It's quite imposing, isn't it? I nursed a Mrs Ogilvie in the hospital a few months ago. She was very sweet.'

'And rich, I suppose,' Makeda suggested, turning away.

'Oh, very rich. Her room was always full of flowers.'

Makeda went through to the kitchen, wondering if the 'very rich' and 'very sweet' lady could possibly be Grant Ogilvie's wife.

In that case, how dared he have touched her, caressing her cheek with the back of his hand as he had done, confusing her and making her hesitate when Jacinthe had asked her to describe him?

CHAPTER TWO

EARLY the following morning Makeda climbed back over the Bluff to look down into Green Turtle Bay. The ketch was still anchored there, although they had seen nothing of its owner at Succoth the previous afternoon. Grant Ogilvie had evidently decided not to intrude on their privacy and had stayed where he was.

She walked back through the scrub, trying to imagine how the valley between the Bluff and Pelican Head had looked when Crichton's had been a thriving plantation house and they had grown sugar down there, and spices. Now there was nothing left of the old elegance but the outline of a ruined mill and the foundations of the huts which had clustered near the shore. The larger settlement at Pelican Head, which Mammy called 'the village', supplied them with all the fish they needed when the boats came in, but it was much too small to support a thriving community. What Millo needed was a blood-transfusion, she supposed, money poured into it to bring it back to its former glory. She had told Grant Ogilvie in no uncertain terms that it would be spoilt by exploiting it as a holiday paradise, but she supposed that what was really happening was that Millo was dying.

Returning to Succoth, she found the house deserted except for Ben and the children, who were making a great noise chasing the chickens in the back yard.

'That ol' rooster he jus' gone clean mad,' Ben informed her. 'He chase all de ducks clean into de scrub!'

'You'll have to find them, Ben, before Mammy comes home.' It was Mammy's day for 'the village'. 'She'll skin you alive for not shutting him up in the pen.'

Ben rolled his eyes.

'Yo' speak true, Miss Makeda. Yo' speak ver' true!' he agreed. 'Ah go find them ducks right away.'

The children ran after him and Makeda was left to her work. Her typewriter was kept in a small room at the back of the house dignified by the name of the study where her father had produced the first rough draft of his book and she had pored over his precious notes in his absence in order to have them sorted out for his return. Affectionately she thought of him as a 'dear' muddler' who never remembered from one day to the next where he had put anything, but now the room seemed almost too tidy. She had come to the end of her material and could do very little more until she received his final batch of notes.

Restlessly she paced between the window and the door. Supposing there weren't any notes to follow those she already had? The idea was unthinkable, yet there had been no definite word from the London solicitors as far as she knew. Her mother had gone to Barbados with the trader a week ago, but when Dolly arrived 'in town' there was no knowing how long she would stay there. The trader was due in again in two days' time, so she supposed she would have to possess her soul in patience until Dolly arrived.

For the next hour she typed industriously, anxious not to waste time, but finally the sound of voices on the verandah broke her concentration and she went through the deserted house to find Grant Ogilvie sitting on one of the long cane chairs being entertained by Jacinthe and Abi.

'Oh——!' She paused in the doorway as he got to his feet. 'I had no idea,' she said in sudden confusion.

'Otherwise you would have rushed to greet me,' he suggested sardonically. 'I came to ask if anyone would like a trip to Barbados,' he added, 'and Abi assures me that it would be much nicer than going back with the trader.'

'I thought you would like to go and have a word with Mr Pettigrew about Father's notes,' Abi said. 'You've been moaning about having nothing to do all week, and Mother might just *not* come with the trader, after all.'

Makeda frowned, not quite knowing what to say. Abi

seemed to have made a friend of Grant Ogilvie already and Jacinthe was feasting her eyes on him as if she had never seen a personable male before. Quiet Jacinthe!

'Mr Pettigrew would write to me if he had anything to deliver,' she answered, 'or Mother would bring the notes.'

'You said yesterday that you couldn't wait to get your hands on them,' Abi reminded her. 'I have to go back with the trader, anyway. My leave is up—unfortunately.' She smiled in Grant's direction. 'I would much rather go on *Seafarer*,' she assured him prettily.

'We could all go,' said Heber, coming in at that moment with the drinks he had mixed. 'Provided we're invited.' He looked across the verandah at Grant, whom he seemed to like. 'It's up to you.'

'*Seafarer* is big enough,' Grant agreed, accepting the tall glass which Heber offered him. 'There's no reason why you shouldn't be my guests.' He looked out of the corner of his eye in Makeda's direction.

'You couldn't hold me back!' Abi laughed. 'And Jacinthe is just dying to go. We could contact Mother and you could come home with the trader on Friday morning.'

Makeda glanced at their unexpected visitor. Was he about to suggest his own return to the island?

'I've some business in Bridgetown,' he said. 'It may keep me there for several days.'

Which effectively ruled out the return trip, Makeda thought.

'Well, Sheba?' Grant's smile was amused. 'What is it to be?'

'I'd—like to go.' She met his eyes steadily enough. 'We're waiting for word from my father's solicitors in Bridgetown to find out if I can continue my work on his book, so perhaps I would gain more time if I saw Mr Pettigrew in person,' she added. 'It might save an exchange of letters, at least.'

Grant drained his rum sour, replacing the glass on the tray.

'How soon can you be ready?' he asked, consulting the watch strapped to his wrist. 'It's ten o'clock. Could you make it by eleven? I can bring *Seafarer* round into the Cove in the meantime, if you wouldn't object.'

He had glanced at Makeda with a wicked gleam in his eyes, but she would not rise to the bait.

'We'll be ready,' Abi assured him. 'You've no idea how quickly we can pack our bags!'

Jacinthe was already at the door, the colour high in her cheeks.

'I'll go and tell Mammy what's happening,' Makeda offered. 'She should be back from the village by now.'

'Think of all the crane chub we'll be missing!' Heber grinned, diving for the long window of his own room which led directly on to the verandah.

They had left the island behind and were sailing north-east towards Barbados by eleven o'clock. It had all happened so quickly that Makeda had hardly taken time to think, but if they had put themselves under an obligation to Grant Ogilvie he hardly seemed to notice the fact.

A brisk wind blowing steadily across their quarter propelled them swiftly along as they left Bequia to starboard and Grant took Heber into the wheelhouse with him to talk about their varied experiences sailing around the Antilles. They were getting on like a house on fire, Makeda observed as she sat beside Jacinthe on the forward deck.

'It's fun, isn't it?' her cousin said dreamily. 'Going to Barbados like this.'

'I'm going for a very definite reason,' Makeda assured her. 'Somehow I know that my father's notes will be there for me to pick up.'

'You're desperately keen to finish his book, aren't you?' said Jacinthe. 'It's like saying "Thank you" to him for all the past.'

'That's exactly how I feel,' Makeda acknowledged with a sudden lump in her throat.

'And yet you weren't all that eager to let Grant Ogilvie help,' Jacinthe pointed out, cupping her chin in the palm of her hand as the wind blew over them. 'Why do you distrust him?'

32

'I didn't know it showed,' said Makeda. 'I don't know him well enough to actually distrust him. It's just that I wouldn't like him to come to Millo or Pelican and change everything.'

Jacinthe turned over on to her side.

'Did he say he was coming?' she asked cautiously.

'Not exactly. He just said that he might be interested, so I suppose he was just snooping around.' Makeda hesitated. 'I suppose I told him in no uncertain manner that he wouldn't be welcome on Millo and it didn't exactly endear me to him.'

'He wouldn't make an issue of a thing like that,' Jacinthe decided. 'He would probably think it merely childish. Oh, I'm sorry, Makeda,' she added contritely. 'I didn't mean to be rude!'

'You weren't,' Makeda laughed, 'because it's perfectly true. I *was* behaving like a wilful child, since the island is no longer our exclusive property any more.'

Jacinthe's eyes darkened.

'It will be like tearing ourselves in two,' she said, 'going away from Millo for good.'

They closed their eyes, allowing the sun to beat down on their golden skins as the lively trade wind blew over them, each thinking their separate thoughts until a shadow fell across them and Makeda sat up with a start. Grant Ogilvie was standing by the forward mast looking down on them.

'All hands below decks!' he commanded 'Abi needs some help in the galley.'

'I'm sorry,' Makeda apologised. 'I didn't mean to laze around.'

'Don't feel too guilty,' he said with a humorous smile. 'You can work your passage by whipping up a meal out of a couple of tins. I'm running out of stores.'

'I brought some fruit.' Makeda hoisted herself to her feet, ignoring the helping hand he had extended. 'And there's some of Mammy's bread-cake. If we get to Barbados by four o'clock,' she added, 'I might just be able to see Mr Pettigrew before he leaves his office.'

He searched her anxious face.

'Why not, when there's so little time to spare?' he said briefly. 'Your father's notes mean a great deal to you, Sheba, but you should be prepared for a disappointment, all the same. I understand from Heber that he was on a pretty tight schedule on this final dig, wanting to achieve as much as possible before the money ran out.'

'Money has always been his main problem,' she found herself confessing. 'Or, at least, the lack of it. It was his colleague, Professor Hunt, who subsidised this final expedition, although my father would want to contribute his share.'

'Hence the sale of Millo,' he reflected, his brows drawn in a tight frown.

'In a way.'

'Money can be the very devil,' he commented.

'Or the lack of it,' she was quick to point out. 'I know it must have been a great sacrifice for him to sell our home, but—but my mother never really liked the life on Millo. The island was too remote and, after Heber went to college, she became very restless. I suppose what he was really trying to do was to provide for us all fairly and I have no right to feel deprived.'

Grant Ogilvie considered her as he walked along the deck in her wake.

'What will you do if there are no more notes to work on?' he asked abruptly.

'I don't know. Look for a job on Barbados, I suppose.'

'As somebody's secretary? I can't quite see you in the rôle of an office slave. You like the open air; you love to sail and have your privacy, but most of all you love Millo. I can only wish you a nice fat little batch of notes to carry you happily into the future,' he concluded.

'I'm not thinking very much beyond finishing my father's book,' she told him, making her way to the galley where, years ago, it seemed, he had brewed cocoa for her in a huge mug and given her a wheaten biscuit to eat.

The green hump of Barbados appeared above the eastern horizon as they finished their meal and they were moored in the yacht basin by three o'clock. It had been a record crossing, with the wind in their favour all the way, Grant told them, picking up Abi's excess baggage to carry it ashore for her.

'I'm going straight to the solicitor's,' Makeda announced. 'Try to contact Mother at St James and I'll meet you there at six o'clock.'

'Do you want me to come with you?' Heber asked.

Makeda shook her head.

'I'd rather go alone, but you can take my grip along to the hotel, if you like. Mother's sure to be there at this time of day.'

Abi was looking pointedly in Grant's direction.

'Shall we see you again?' she asked. 'We'll be at Waldon's Hotel till Friday, I expect.'

Grant considered the invitation while Heber found a taxi.

'I won't make any rash promises,' he said. 'I've got a lot of loose ends to tie up, businesswise, and I may have to fly over to Antigua for a few days to inspect some building land.'

'For another hotel?' Abi laughed. 'Is there no end to your property empire, or are you going to build a house for your own pleasure, this time?'

'Not on Antigua,' he assured her. 'I have a completely different idea.'

Makeda had signalled her own taxi.

'Goodbye,' she said, holding out her hand. 'I doubt if we'll meet again, so—thanks for everything.'

Grant held her fingers in a vice-like grip for a moment, and it seemed as if he was about to say something of importance, but instead he set her free.

'Good luck, Sheba!' he said. 'I hope you'll find what you're searching for before very long.'

The taxi-cab was crossing Trafalgar Square and turning into Broad Street before she had gathered her scattered thoughts together. He had wished her good luck, but not goodbye.

The offices of Messrs Gothram, Tynedall & Pettigrew were situated above a bank on a corner half-way along Broad Street, and she paid off the cab and rushed up the familiar

35

stairway to arrive, breathless, at the heavy glass door with the firm's name on it. Smoothing her hair, she enquired in the outer office for Mr Pettigrew, who was now the senior partner and an old friend.

'It's rather urgent,' she explained. 'I've come across from Millo specially to see him.'

The rather severe-looking woman clerk took her message into an inner office and almost immediately an elderly man with a grey beard and twinkling blue eyes appeared in the doorway.

'Makeda, my dear child!' he exclaimed. 'We haven't met for a very long time.' His friendly scrutiny took in the blue linen dress she wore almost awkwardly and the thick auburn hair falling loosely on her shoulders. She had released it from its confining rubber bands, allowing it to swing free, and the effect, as far as James Pettigrew was concerned, was charming. She was John Garland's daughter all right, he mused, naïve, perhaps, when she was forced to account for herself in a sophisticated community, but hardly a fool. He had seen her through most of her childhood and her adolescence, approving her education and her affection for the one parent who really cared about her, and now he was prepared to see her past another milestone along the road to the future.

'I came about my father's book,' Makeda told him as he settled her in the chair beside his desk. 'Have the notes come, Mr Pettigrew? Have they been sent from London?'

'They're on their way,' he assured her. 'I told your mother when she was here this morning to let you know, but I gather you haven't seen her yet?'

'No. I came straight from the Yacht Club,' Makeda explained. 'The whole family are here now. Someone gave us a lift.'

He studied her closely.

'You won't be familiar with the terms of your father's will, in that case,' he remarked. 'I'll sketch them for you as briefly as I can.'

'I'm only concerned about the notes,' Makeda told him. 'I have to finish his book.'

'I understand that, and you would like to finish it on the island.'

'I couldn't think of anything I would like better.'

She looked down at her clenched hands, noticing how brown they were with constant immersion in the sea, like a beach urchin's.

'Your father sold the lease on Millo some time ago,' the lawyer was saying. 'But you already knew that, I believe. It was the only way open to him to provide for you if anything was to happen to him in Saudi Arabia, and it also gave him the satisfaction of paying his share during the excavations. Professor Hunt bought Millo mainly to help him out, and your father has divided the remainder of the money very fairly among you all. He knew you wanted to stay on Millo, Makeda, but it wasn't possible. He had his commitments to the rest of the family and to your mother.'

'Yes,' Makeda agreed, 'I've got to accept that, haven't I? Jacinthe and I were the only ones who wanted to stay on the island.'

'Your father has provided for Jacinthe, too,' the lawyer said. 'It is all very fair and reasonable, my dear. He could not favour one at the expense of the others.'

'I wouldn't have expected that,' she said quickly, 'and I suppose I knew I couldn't stay on Millo for ever, no matter how much I wanted to, but I thought we would be safe there so long as Professor Hunt was the new owner. He admired my father so much and they worked well together. They had the same objective, the same plans.'

Mr Pettigrew cleared his throat.

'It was an ideal situation where you and your father were concerned,' he agreed. 'The covenant in their contract which allowed Succoth to remain your father's home as long as he needed it was a very generous one.'

'And now they're both dead and someone else will buy the lease,' Makeda suggested. 'Unless the Professor has an heir.'

She waited almost painfully for the lawyer's answer.

'Professor Hunt was a bachelor, as you know.' James Pettigrew rose to take a bundle of papers from the filing cabinet between the two long windows. 'But he did leave an heir.'

Makeda leaned forward in her chair, the colour draining slowly from her cheeks.

'A nephew,' the lawyer added. 'His sister's son.'

Makeda's eyes were suddenly full of tears.

'Oh, Mr Pettigrew,' she cried, 'it's worse than I thought! This young man will probably put the island on the market again and *anyone* could buy it.'

'I don't think you need worry on that account,' James Pettigrew told her kindly. 'Grant Ogilvie has other plans for Millo. He doesn't mean to sell.'

She stared at him across the desk.

'Grant Ogilvie?' she repeated. 'It can't be true! He brought us over from Millo and he never said a word about why he was there. He listened to our confidences without divulging one single fact about himself which would have put us on our guard.'

'It's true enough.' James Pettigrew tapped the sheaf of papers he had taken from the cabinet. 'It's all here in a codicil to the professor's will.'

When she had regained her breath Makeda said slowly:

'He won't be right for Millo, Mr Pettigrew. He means to change it. I'm certain of that. He's a property developer and all he wants to do is to add Millo to his existing empire.'

The old man shook his head.

'We mustn't cross too many bridges before we come to them,' he advised. 'As a matter of fact, Mr Ogilvie has agreed to honour his uncle's commitment. You needn't leave Millo till your father's book is finished.'

It was what she wanted, it was the chance to finish her half-completed work in peace, yet there was a storm of protest in her heart when she thought of Millo being despoiled under her very eyes.

'I couldn't bear it!' she cried passionately. 'Being there while he built holiday chalets or a great towering hotel at Green Turtle Bay! Oh, I know it's selfish of me to feel like this,' she acknowledged, 'but Millo has always been *my* island and there was so much for me to do there.'

'Why not swallow your pride and accept Mr Ogilvie's offer, in that case?' James Pettigrew suggested mildly. 'I know you're dedicated to finishing your father's book and I think he would have expected it of you, Makeda. I know everyone is searching for King Solomon's Mines, but your father had another idea. Probably that's why you were called Makeda,' he mused.

'You mean that there were other mines?'

'Of course. You may remember that the Queen of Sheba also brought gold and precious stones to Solomon when she came to visit him. The question is from where?'

'Do you think my father and George Hunt made some sort of discovery?' she asked eagerly. 'There's nothing in the first batch of notes to suggest that they actually found a new mine.'

'It could have happened,' said the old lawyer. 'Many people have concentrated on such a find in the past, riches beyond the dreams of avarice, and there could be some indication of it in the notes we're waiting for.' He paused expectantly. 'A hidden message, perhaps, an indication of the exact location if a mine had been found.'

Makeda shook her head, although her cheeks were flushed and her eyes very bright.

'It's too sensational,' she declared. 'My father has always rejected fantasy.'

'Invention or not,' the lawyer responded, 'how can we assess it when so little is really known about these things? When will you finish the MS? I believe Andresson & Marks are very keen to have it in their hands before the autumn for publication next year.'

'I'll do my best to finish it as quickly as possible,' she promised, 'now that I can go on working at Succoth without the upheaval of having to find somewhere else to live in the meantime.'

'And then?' he asked.

'I haven't thought beyond that book,' she had to confess. 'I don't want to leave Millo, but I know I shall have to go.'

'What about your mother and Heber? I know Abi's nicely placed in New York.'

'Heber has another year to do at college and Mother will look at all this as a merciful release.' There was no use beating about the bush, especially with James Pettigrew, who was well aware of the situation which her father had come to terms with in his own unobtrusive way. 'Jacinthe has finished school now, but I don't think she has decided what to do.'

'Nurse, probably,' the lawyer suggested. 'You're all protected by your father's will and your education will be completed, as he desired.'

'Because he sold Millo!' she cried. 'Oh, I don't mean to sound so bitter, but had he to do it, Mr Pettigrew?'

'It was done a long time ago, to help with your own education, although George Hunt did nothing about taking possession,' the old man explained. 'It was a way of helping a friend and subsidising their research. Your father was determined to bear his fair share of the expedition and George Hunt had already started to build his Caribbean empire. Land was the obvious way to invest his money, and he left the development of it to his nephew.'

Makeda didn't want to speak about Grant Ogilvie. She had said her say, but the hurt over Millo remained, deep in her heart. Not even nice kind Mr Pettigrew could understand the distress and pain she felt at the thought of her loss. Millo had been her home for so long, her secret island where she had dreamed a thousand dreams and most of them had come true. There was freedom there, and beauty, and the poignant memory of the past when she had worked tirelessly with her father, sharing his enthusiasm at a new find when he had returned to tell her about it.

The work they had shared was not yet at an end, but the island was no longer secure. She rose to her feet.

'I won't keep you any longer, Mr Pettigrew,' she said. 'I know you must be ready to go home, but perhaps I could come back tomorrow to see if the notes have arrived?'

'Leave it till the afternoon,' he suggested. 'Will you go back to the island on Friday?'

'With the trader,' she nodded. 'Mother will probably come with us. It must be expensive living in a hotel all this time.'

'She has many friends in Bridgetown,' James Pettigrew reflected. 'She may even settle over here for a while.'

'Yes.' It would be the solution to at least one of her mother's dreams. She would be in the social swim, at least for a year until Heber graduated. 'What time tomorrow?'

'About three o'clock. I should have sorted through the mail by then.'

The lawyer walked with her to the outer door, aware of her abstraction as they shook hands and wondering if there was any way in which he could help. Makeda was young and intense, yet he knew her to be sensible enough. All the same, this had been a big disappointment for her, coming so swiftly on her father's death, this leaving Millo, which was her true home. He shook his head as he thought about Dolly Garland.

'I feel I should have good news for you tomorrow,' he said before they parted. 'Your father's London solicitors spoke of a quantity of valuable notes.'

Makeda's heart lifted as she went swiftly down the stairs. At least she had the excitement of her work to fall back on and the chance to complete it at Succoth.

Travelling out along Highway One, she realised that they had come to Barbados at Carnival time. It was Crop Over, and the festival was already in full swing. The month-long Bajan fête was the biggest event of the year, with its richly-packed programme of artistic, cultural and sporting events based upon the historic forms of merrymaking on the old plantations of the post-emancipation era. Her mother loved the excitement of Crop Over, although it was now a big, noisy, crowded event far and away removed from the one-day rejoicings on the original plantations, when the workers drove to the local mill decked out with bright flowers and gay ribbons to celebrate the fact that the crop was over and the cane harvest safely gathered in.

Lavishly-decorated floats jammed the carriageways in their

41

efforts to return to the town centre, while the milling crowd made swift progress impossible. The bus was surrounded again and again by singing, gesticulating Bajans in holiday attire, while other more intrepid characters who had climbed on to the ledges of buildings pelted the decorated carts with bougainvillea, Pride of Barbados and hibiscus until the carriageway looked like some vast floral carpet stretching away along the coast.

The crushed, decapitated blossoms made Makeda turn her head away, although she knew that there were millions of flowers on the island.

St James had staged its own Crop Over attractions with folk-singing and dancing, drama, arts and crafts demonstrations and traditional feasting at most of the hotels, but Waldon's was amazingly quiet when she finally reached it. She glanced at her watch. It was six o'clock, yet nobody seemed to be around waiting with a cool drink in their hand before they went up to dress for dinner.

'Everyone is out at some sort of exhibition or another,' the smiling proprietress told her. 'Your mother and brother are having dinner privately, with some friends.' She turned to the rows of pigeonholes behind her. 'You'll need the key to your room,' she suggested, 'so you can change.'

'I'm not going out,' Makeda said, feeling strangely neglected. 'I came over on business.'

'Oh, but you mustn't think of business at Crop Over!' the proprietress insisted. 'It's a time for relaxation, for gaiety and fun. Surely you have someone to take you into town?'

'Only my brother,' Makeda smiled, 'and he has apparently got other ideas. Do you know if Abi and Jacinthe went with them?'

'I can't be sure. I didn't see them go out, but I think they left a message in your room.' The proprietress handed over the key. 'If you really would prefer to stay in I can let you have supper here later on,' she offered. 'It may not be up to our usual menu because everyone is out, but we'll do our best.'

'A sandwich will be enough,' Makeda assured her. 'I'm not very hungry.'

Her last meal had been on board *Seafarer*, a scratch affair which she had helped Abi to prepare, but they had all enjoyed it, sitting out on deck with the sun on their faces and the wind blowing through their hair.

The memory took her thoughts back to Grant Ogilvie, who had looked so supremely confident standing with his back to the sea and his eyes fixed on the billowing sails. Something of Henry Morgan and a dozen other pirates was etched on his dark face as his eyes had ranged across the incredible expanse of blue ocean between them and their destination. Was he thinking, even then, of the island he had inherited and the irritating complications of his uncle's will?

Her room was at the back of the hotel overlooking a pleasant garden, with bougainvillea wandering across the high wall which surrounded it and an enormous flamboyant crowding out most of the other trees. She remembered the small patio leading out of the downstairs hall, supposing that she could take her belated evening meal out there when the time came.

An envelope addressed in her mother's neat handwriting was propped against her dressing-mirror and she opened it without a great deal of curiosity, reading the short note it contained as she sat on the end of the single bed.

'We've gone to the Ashfords' for the evening,' her mother wrote. 'Come if you like. They're putting on a gala dinner for a few friends in the old plantation style. Nothing spectacular, you understand. Just dinner and dancing at the plantation yard with the traditional entertainment. We're so tired of all the noise and revelry in Bridgetown and it's quite impossible to shop. Abi hasn't very much time before she goes off to New York, so this will be a nice change for her.'

There was no mention of Jacinthe, but it was almost certain that she would be at the Ashfords' with the others.

Makeda took off her crumpled blue linen smock to stand under the shower while she decided what to do. 'Come if you like!' It was a cold sort of bidding and one she could not quite appreciate in her present state of mind. Her mother had known the Ashfords for years and was hopeful that Heber would eventually marry one of their daughters, but none of the Ashford women were really Makeda's type. They were all conventionally fashionable, going to the 'right' parties and attending the regattas, gymkhanas and balls authorised by their parents, who had very definite plans for their futures. None of them appeared to have any personality of their own. Abi had struck up a friendship with Roger Ashford which Dolly approved in an offhand sort of way, wondering if two Ashfords in the family was really possible. They were old plantation stock, proud of their ancestry to the point of being boring about it, and they lived in a grand house on the outskirts of Bridgetown which was more like a museum than a home.

I don't really want to go, Makeda concluded, picking up her grip from the floor where Heber had left it.

Now, she said to herself with a puckish gleam in her eyes, to dress for dinner! What shall I wear? My too-short cotton with the tiered skirt or the cream silk Abi grew out of a year ago?

She held up the green cotton dress which was hopelessly crushed, so there was no alternative but the cream-coloured silk two-piece which her mother had bought for Abi when she had passed her exams.

I wonder if cream and me really go together, she thought, gazing at her reflection in the inadequate looking-glass on the far wall. Her hair was still wet from the shower, clinging in damp tendrils about her brow, and her eyes were enormous. Strange eyes, she mused critically, neither blue nor green, with odd little golden flecks in them like sun dancing on water on a clear day.

The two-piece was expensively simple and it did not show her knees. She felt ladylike and prim, going down to dinner in an unfashionable hotel all on her own with no one to admire her but the hotel cat.

At the first bend in the staircase she drew up. Someone was standing in the middle of the hall, a tall, black-browed man whom she could not fail to recognise, although his powerful body was now clad in a light tropical suit and his hair was neatly brushed.

Grant Ogilvie! She drew away from the ornate gilt banisters, leaning back against the wall in the hope that he would not look up and discover her, but in the next instant she realised how foolish that was. He had only to enquire at the reception desk to find out that she had booked in less than an hour ago and was probably still in her room.

Gripping the large canvas sac which was the only handbag she possessed, she walked steadily down the stairs to confront him, supposing that he had come to find Abi since it was her sister who had extended the invitation to him as they left the yacht club. He had been standing with his back turned to the staircase, but he swung round immediately at her approach. She had covered half of the tessellated floor, reducing the distance between them, when he said:

'What in heaven's name have you got in the bag? The Crown Jewels?'

'It's the only bag I have,' she defended the incongruous-looking sac. 'Besides, I like it. It holds everything.'

'Apparently!' His eyes took in the elegant cream suit. 'But it does nothing for the total effect. Are you going out?'

It was impossible to tell him anything but the truth.

'No. I'm going to have a sandwich on the patio later on.'

'And in the meantime?'

'I can read a book.' Her eyes were greener than he had imagined. 'There's plenty of them lying around.'

'Where are the others—Heber and Abi and your cousin?' he asked.

'They've gone to a party. A private one.'

'What happened to you?'

'I was late getting back. I'd forgotten about Crop Over, and the buses were crowded.'

'Surely you could have taken a taxi?'

'The end result would have been the same, and I haven't that sort of money.'

He allowed the half-snub to pass him by.

'Have you eaten since *Seafarer*?' he asked.

'No. I don't want anything to eat.'

'Isn't that rather a childish reaction to the remark about the bag?' He fixed her with an eagle look. 'I want to talk to you about Millo.'

'Because you know I've been to the lawyer's and found out who you really are?'

He came a step nearer.

'I haven't had much opportunity to tell you about myself,' he said. 'You've always taken the initiative when it came to Millo, making any wildly inaccurate accusation which took your fancy.' He put a firm hand under her elbow, propelling her towards the door. 'We can't discuss this in a hotel lobby,' he added briskly. 'If we have a lot to say to each other it had better be done in some sort of privacy.'

'I've told you I don't want a meal,' she protested, attempting to free herself.

'And I'm starving. It will take us at least an hour to get back into town, so you may have regained your appetite by then.'

'I couldn't go without a scarf,' she said, playing for time to adjust her scattered thoughts.

'I'll give you five minutes,' he said.

Makeda ran back up the stairs, two at a time, reaching her bedroom door in a state of breathlessness. Why had he decided to take up Abi's invitation so quickly? Why had he come just at that moment when she had been about to make her escape into the garden? The chances were that she could have remained undetected out there while he enquired for her brother or Abi and she needn't have undergone the humiliation of meeting him quite so soon. She was still confused and angry at the revelation of his true identity and the fact that he had landed on Millo without contacting them beforehand. He had come like a thief in the night, she told herself, to spy out the land, and now he was saying: 'I want to talk to you about Millo'.

Was he about to deliver some harsh sort of ultimatum concerning the duration of their stay at Succoth, handing out largesse with one hand while he took everything else away

46

with the other? All her love for her island home surged up within her while the tears which she was determined not to shed glinted in her green eyes.

I'll tell him what I think, she decided, catching up the fine woollen scarf which Mammy had knitted for her as a birthday present. It was like a cobweb, as fine as lace, and it was meant to be worn as both head-covering and shoulder-drape, but Makeda thrust it into the utilitarian capaciousness of the rough linen sac with a determined tightening of her jaw. Grant Ogilvie had been laughing at her when he had denounced the sac, but she did not care. Her only reason for accepting his on-the-spot invitation was to find out more about what he meant to do with Millo.

'I'm ready,' she announced when she reached the hall and found him chatting to the proprietress.

'I've told Mrs Burgess you won't be back for supper,' he told her.

Short of creating a scene, which Sophie Burgess would have relished, she could hardly contradict him. Instead, she said:

'I won't be late. If my mother and the rest of the family come back early, Mrs Burgess, will you tell them where I've gone?'

'Where *are* you going?' Sophie asked with an expectant smile. 'There's so much to chose from at carnival time.'

'We'll play it by ear,' Grant told her as a hire-car drew up at the door. 'Ready?' He turned towards Makeda.

Her fingers tightened on the canvas sac, as if she expected him to comment on it again, but he held open the car door and she got into the front passenger seat.

'I prefer to drive myself,' he explained when they had dropped the native chauffeur in Holetown. 'Where would you like to go?'

'It's years since I've been to Crop Over,' she said, relaxing against the comfortable cushioning of the passenger seat. 'The festivities have grown enormously since we were here last.'

Remembering her previous visit to Bridgetown with her father as her companion, she was silent for a moment.

'What's the matter?' her companion asked. 'Wishing you hadn't come?'

'Something like that. What did you want to say to me, Mr Ogilvie?'

'It'll keep,' he decided, smiling at her conventional use of his name. 'The carnival spirit is building up. I have to give all my attention to the road.'

They had reached the outskirts of the town where the crowds were already thickening. It seemed that the whole of Barbados was on joyful holiday, dancing and singing in the streets, greeting one another, watching the various contests and listening to the steel bands. In the Bay the *Jolly Roger* was waiting to take off on her evening cruise into the silky darkness, her scarlet sails lit from below by huge brass lanterns, the skull-and-crossbones flag prominent on her aftermast. Her pirate crew were already aboard, singing as they waited to sail off into the darkness, and the glow of yellow lights shone out from her cabins through leaded widows, like friendly stars against the deepening blue of the sky.

'I love it!' Makeda exclaimed involuntarily. 'Nothing has been overlooked. It *is* the past!'

'Which you prefer to the present?' Grant Ogilvie suggested.

'I was perfectly happy in the present.'

'Until I came along?' His tone was sardonic. 'There are some things we have to live with, Sheba, however painful they may seem.'

'Like losing the present?' She bit her lip to keep it steady.

'And like growing up.' His dark profile was etched against the gay background of the crowd-filled street. 'We all have to come to terms with that contingency, sooner or later. I reached the starting point a long time ago.'

'You talk as if you were ninety!' she exclaimed. 'How old were you when you started to build your empire?'

He smiled at her choice of words.

'Not more than twenty,' he answered. 'I inherited most of it from my uncle. The professor was a man of many parts, as you may know. He bought land to develop it, but his chief interest was the work he did with your father. I owe him a great deal,' he added simply. 'He brought me up, you see, when my own father died, and I always wanted to repay him in some way. As far as I could see, the only way was to look after his property interests while he was abroad.'

Makeda had been watching him as he spoke, faintly astonished by his confession because he had seemed too hard for sentiment, too much the man of the world to think of returning loyalty where kindness had been given.

'Were you very young when you were orphaned?' she asked.

'My mother lived for several years after my father, but she was ill most of the time, in and out of hospital in New York and in great pain with an arthritic spine. I was twenty-five when she died, the age of responsibility, but it still hit me like a blow between the eyes.'

'Are you married?' she asked bluntly, remembering Abi's reference to 'the very rich and very sweet' Mrs Ogilvie whom she had nursed when she had first gone to New York. 'No, I don't suppose you are,' she added hastily when he didn't answer her immediately. 'Otherwise you wouldn't be sailing around the Caribbean on your own.'

He laughed outright.

'I sail around on my own because *Seafarer* has been my only home for the past two years,' he explained. 'I have everything I need aboard her, as you no doubt discovered for yourself.'

'When I "snooped around", you mean.' She was thinking about her impetuous swim out to the ketch as it lay at anchor in Green Turtle Bay.

'When I invited you aboard,' he corrected. 'What do you think of her?' he asked.

'She's beautiful. The perfect sailing ship!'

He looked pleased, accepting her unstinted praise like the mariner he undoubtedly was.

'How long have you had her?'

'Four years. She replaced a very old schooner I used to charter to earn a living when I first came to the Caribbean. I sailed out of Antigua in those days,' he added reminiscently as they were held up by a group of chanting Bajans marching ahead of a steel band.

'You've been here a long time,' she reflected, 'and I suppose you mean to stay.'

'Undoubtedly.' The street lights, augmented by flares, lit up his dark face. 'There is no other place.'

'And Millo?' she asked, her voice unsteady.

'I have my plans for Millo,' he said, 'although I expect Mr Pettigrew told you that you needn't be turned out of Succoth immediately.'

'Yes.'

She sat back in her seat, some of the magic going out of the scene before her. It all boiled down to Millo in the end!

Grant drove towards the bay.

'The Holiday Inn, or somewhere quieter?' he queried.

'I'm not grand enough for the Inn,' she told him hastily, thinking that she would be like a fish out of water among the more sophisticated of the island revellers. 'Perhaps you can think of somewhere less exotic?'

He turned the car immediately.

'Would you like to go out to Cattlewash?' he asked. 'There's a place there right on the cliff edge I think you'd enjoy. It's not at all pretentious,' he added with a faint smile, 'and one can talk without being deafened by calypso.'

They drove swiftly along Highway Three to Blackman's and over Horse Hill to Joe's River, dropping down to the East Coast Road at Bathsheba where the Altantic came bounding in to break on the rocks far below. It was the other face of Barbados, rugged in places and grim, but it held its own fascination after the noisy, crowded streets of Bridgetown.

The wind was stronger here, a rollicking wind which buffeted them as they made their way across the carpark attached to the spectacular little restaurant poised on the edge of the cliff. There was carnival here, too, but on a more subdued scale, and they were immediately accommodated at a corner table overlooking the ocean.

'It's like being on the bridge of a ship!' Makeda exclaimed, facing her companion across the lamplit table. 'And all that wind has given me an appetite.'

He ordered for them both, assured that nothing but the best would be served to them because he appeared to be quite well known on this more remote side of the island.

'What are you going to drink?' he asked. 'Lemonade?'

She recognised the teasing note in his voice, but this time she smiled.

'I'm going to have something quite exotic,' she decided, 'since it's Carnival.'

'Don't overdo it,' he cautioned. 'I want to talk to you.'

It was as if he had deliberately poured cold water on her enthusiasm, although he continued to smile across the table into her eyes.

'Can we leave our talk till afterwards?' she asked.

'Enjoy your dinner,' he answered with a shrug, 'now that you've found an appetite.'

The meal was exquisite, served in true Bajan style by dusky waiters in short white coats and dark trousers who beamed on them benevolently as each set of plates was changed for the next. Delicious fruit and coffee completed the five-course meal, and Makeda sat back gazing at her amused companion with a sense of wellbeing as the local 'Took Band' began to play.

The music was very dear to her, a part of the Islands she was never likely to forget, and far nearer to the heart of the people than the more popular calypso. It was true Crop Over, something which had been performed down through the years at the old mills and the molasses terminals when the rich plantation owners had entertained their workers in their own yards. She could almost see the stick-licking and the maypole-plaiting and the acrobatics performed on the greasy pole, and the merry-go-round for the children with its wooden horses and jaunty little cars.

Two masked figures came in to dance in the centre of the floor, gyrating to the sound of the kettle-drum and flute, their feather headdresses jangling with dozens of colourful beads as they whirled among the tables. Makeda watched with parted lips, her eyes glowing in the lamplight because she had forgotten about Millo for a moment.

Then, when the inevitable calypso was announced and the air was full of the sound of twanging guitars, Grant Ogilvie led her on to the dance floor. The arms that went round her were as strong as steel and the lights and the music were suddenly meant for her alone. Grant held her close because there was so little room on the floor and for a moment she wondered if he could actually feel the wild and uncontrollable beating of her foolish heart. Because it was foolishness to imagine that anything so commonplace as a dance to the music of calypso could possibly stir him to the mad response she was feeling as she circled the floor in his arms.

When the last twanging note died in the silence and before he let her go he pressed his lips to her forehead in an offhand little kiss.

'Sheba,' he said, 'you really do love all this. You're quite a child.'

She walked ahead of him across the floor.

'You dance very well yourself,' she said, determined to ignore the kiss. 'Is it something you've always done?'

'Not for a long time.' He was looking down at her with an odd expression in his eyes. 'Did your father send the notes you expected to pick up this afternoon?'

She drew back as if he had struck her. So that was it! He had brought her out here to soften her up, to ask questions and discover something he wanted to know. Something in her recoiled before the thought.

'I didn't pick them up, if that's what you want to know,' she answered frigidly.

'But they are on their way? From London, perhaps?' He leaned across the table towards her. 'I'm asking because I'm really interested,' he said. 'My uncle also took some notes and I wondered if they might be the same.'

She looked into his eyes with something like horror in her own.

'What are you suggesting?' she demanded. 'Do you expect

me to let you see my father's private papers before I've looked at them myself?'

'Not at all.' He dismissed her angry sarcasm with a brief gesture of his hand. 'All I wanted to do was to offer you some more information if my uncle's notes were different from your father's.'

'I can hardly believe you would be so magnanimous,' she said, hurt and angered by the change which had suddenly come over her lovely evening. 'Please take me back to St James. I couldn't bear to stay here a moment longer!'

He summoned their waiter, paying his bill and leaving a generous tip.

'Perhaps a breath of fresh air would do us both good,' he suggested as the restaurant door was opened for them.

'I want to go back right away,' she told him firmly.

'You're sure?' The haunting notes of another calypso drifted out through the open window above their heads.

'I should never have come.'

'Because of the kiss, or because I asked you a simple favour?' He sounded amused.

'It wasn't just a favour,' she cried, ignoring the first part of his question. 'It was something tremendously important.' Her eyes accused him as he helped her into the waiting car. 'My father's notes are something I could never share with anyone. They're too precious to me, quite apart from being essential for his book. I want to finish that book as a—sort of memorial to him, but I don't suppose you would know how I feel.'

He started the engine.

'You're not alone in your desire to perpetuate a memory, Makeda,' he told her sternly. 'I have always wanted to do something for the man who brought me up and this seemed to be it. If my uncle's notes are really no use to you,' he added firmly, 'I shall look at them myself with a view to publishing.'

She drew in a deep, resentful breath.

'You know, of course, that the two books would probably kill each other if they came out simultaneously,' she said.

'I'd have to take that chance. Since you're so far ahead with your father's version I would probably lose out on the transaction,' he added, 'but I wouldn't be in it for the money, contrary to your belief, I imagine.'

'I don't think you need money,' she said as they raced along the road which wound high above the coast. 'You have more than you'll ever be able to use, but I do believe you're impelled by the desire to succeed at whatever you decide to do. You're utterly ruthless in that respect, I fancy, although I hardly know you.'

The final words had been almost a cry of despair and she turned her face away from him towards the sea.

'You're quite right,' he answered slowly. 'You don't know me.'

The journey back across the island seemed never ending, with the moon riding high in the heavens ahead of them and all the hills like papercuts silhouetted against a cloudless sky. Dark patches of trees appeared and disappeared on either side when they finally plunged into a secondary dirt-road which would take them more quickly to their destination, and Makeda drew Mammy's shawl over her head as if to shield herself from some unexpected cold. Yet the night was soft and languid even on the heights surrounding Mount Hillaby, caressing her cheek like the touch of a man's warm lips on her skin.

Carnival was still very much alive on the other side of the island, the white sand beaches thronged with the people who had drifted out from the towns. Torches flared along the paths to the larger hotels, while a myriad of gaily-coloured light bulbs glittered among the palms.

They went down into Holetown and up along the coast, listening to the muted sounds of revelry around the open fires where the barbecues were being prepared. Here and there the flame of limbo glowed beneath the trees as the fireswallowers performed their daring act, and endless couples strolled, hand-in-hand, towards the ocean listening to the calypso of the waves.

Makeda caught the shawl closer to her throat.

'Are you cold?' Grant asked.

'No. I was thinking how far removed all this was from Millo.'

'You have only another day to wait,' he reminded her brusquely, 'if you do mean to return with the trader.'

'I'd like to get back as quickly as possible,' she said stiffly.

They had reached the hotel and he turned the car into the narrow drive to help her out.

'You needn't wait,' she said. 'Nobody appears to be back yet. Certainly not Mother or Abi.'

There were no lights in the upper rooms of the hotel, although a couple of despondent-looking torches flared over the patio on either side of the overgrown flamboyant.

'I'll see you safely in,' Grant decided.

They walked round to the deserted patio, standing for a moment beneath the unsteady flares, the flickering orange light playing on their faces as they looked at each other.

'Thank you for the meal,' Makeda said conventionally. 'It was very kind of you.'

He laughed outright.

'How nicely you say your party-piece, Sheba!' he mocked. 'I can't honestly reply that it's been a pleasure. If you do need my uncle's notes, let me know.'

Before she had turned in at the door he had gone.

CHAPTER THREE

It was long after midnight before the sound of another car broke the silence which had settled over the hotel in the wake of Grant's noisy departure. He had driven the hire-car away with his foot hard down on the throttle and Makeda had followed its progress until it reached the main road.

The second car was chauffeur-driven and must have been put at her mother's disposal by her host. Abi and Jacinthe and Heber spilled out of it, to be followed by her mother, who seemed to be in very high spirits indeed.

'What a really delightful evening!' Makeda heard her say as Heber opened the front door. 'I don't think I fully realised what I've been missing all these years until this evening.'

Makeda's heart felt like a hard, tight lump in her breast. There was no need to speculate about the future as far as her mother was concerned. Dolly's decision about Millo had been succinctly expressed in those few brief words down there on the gravelled terrace while she waited for her son to open the door.

Almost reluctantly Makeda went back downstairs to meet them in the hall.

'Dear me, Makeda!' Dolly greeted her. 'You *do* look as if you've been losing your sleep. Why didn't you come out to the Ashfords'? I left a note.'

'I got it when I came back from the lawyer's,' Makeda told her, 'and by then it seemed rather late to go out to St John's. Mrs Ashford's motto has always been "Punctuality—or else!" '

'You missed a superb dinner, to say nothing of the excellent entertainment. Where have you been?' Dolly noticed the cream silk suit. 'You're quite dressed up.'

'I decided to have a sandwich here,' Makeda began to explain, only to be interrupted by her mother, who was intent on procuring her customary 'nightcap'.

'I suppose Mrs Burgess has gone to bed.' Dolly switched on the drawing-room lights. 'Ah, here we are! She's left a tray.'

'I couldn't eat another bite,' Abi declared. 'Where *did* you go, Makeda?' she asked beneath her breath. 'You wouldn't have worn all that clobber just to eat a solitary sandwich in the patio!'

'I went to Bathsheba with Grant Ogilvie,' Makeda told her. 'He came here at your invitation, remember?'

'The dickens you did!' Abi's eyes were wide with surprise. 'Talk about dark horses! Did he think Bathsheba was highly appropriate?'

'I don't know what he thought, except perhaps that going across to the Atlantic coast might blow some of my cobwebs away.'

Makeda went on into the room where Dolly had ensconced herself on one of the comfortable settees with her feet up. Heber and Jacinthe followed her in.

'Pour out for us, Jacinthe,' she commanded. 'I think you enjoyed yourself quite well this evening. I saw you dancing with the same young man several times. Did you know he was Mrs Ashford's nephew?'

Jacinthe shook her head. She had been close behind them when Abi had challenged Makeda about the cream suit and the mention of Grant Ogilvie's name had sent the colour flying into her cheeks.

'He told me he was from England and I thought he was rather shy.' She answered her aunt's question abstractedly, as if her thoughts were very far away. 'If you don't mind, Aunt Dolly, I'll go upstairs with Abi. I'm rather tired.'

'Tired, at your age!' Dolly exclaimed. 'You young people have no stamina nowadays.' She eased off her shoes. 'When I was your age I frequently danced till morning and never thought a thing about it.'

'You did well enough this evening,' Heber reminded her

dryly. 'Who was the old buffer you were dancing with most of the time?'

Dolly patted her hair into place, glancing at her reflection in the looking-glass on the opposite wall.

'An old friend of Reggie Ashford. He had a position at Government House at one time and has come back to retire here.'

'Do I scent a whiff of romance?' her son enquired, handing over her nightcap.

'Certainly not! You are a tease, Heber,' Dolly declared. 'Sit down and tell me what you've been doing on Millo while I've been away.'

Makeda moved towards the door.

'Don't go!' her mother commanded, sipping her hot rum and molasses. 'I have something to tell you.'

'Something important, or will it keep till breakfast?' Makeda asked.

Her mother swung her feet to the floor.

'It would keep, but there's no reason why you shouldn't hear it now.' Dolly had always revelled in a sense of the dramatic. 'I've had a letter from London from someone who calls himself Simon Wetherby.'

The name sounded familiar, although Makeda failed to place it for a moment.

'He tells me he worked with your father and Professor Hunt in Egypt.'

Makeda turned back into the room, her cheeks faintly flushed, her lips parted in anticipation of some further news. Perhaps Simon Wetherby had been with the last, ill-fated expedition just before her father died. She had felt hurt when her mother had failed to ask about her visit to James Pettigrew's office when they had first met, but perhaps Dolly's mysterious letter from London would explain her seeming indifference.

'Had he anything important to say?' she asked.

'He appears to think that he might be of some use to you while you're finishing the manuscript,' Dolly told her. 'He knew your father was writing a book and he wants to help.'

'I wonder how he could do that,' said Makeda. 'I won't be going to London.'

'He's coming here.' Dolly finished the remainder of her drink. 'I think we ought to invite him to Millo,' she added. 'He seems a very nice young man.'

'Young?'

'His letter *sounded* young. Of course, I don't know,' Dolly conceded. 'He may be as old as your father.'

'He was a geologist,' Makeda remembered. 'Just out of college, I think. That would be four years ago, if he was on the first half of the dig, which makes him around twenty-six.'

'A sensible age,' Dolly declared. 'I've written to say we'll be pleased to see him.'

'On Millo?'

'Where else? Until things are finally settled I shall have to make my home there,' Dolly pointed out. 'Your father's will has left us comfortable and the island has changed hands, but Mr Pettigrew tells me we needn't leave immediately. I don't like to be rushed into things,' she added. 'I want to be quite sure that I'm not making another ghastly mistake.'

Makeda said goodnight.

'We'll have to meet this Simon Wetherby if he gets here before we leave for Millo,' Dolly pointed out. 'You and Heber could go out to Seawell and pick him up with a hire-car. Then we can see what he looks like before we invite him to the island.'

Makeda glanced across the room at her brother, who was topping up his rum sour.

'As long as he doesn't have a long beard and walk about with his pockets full of rocks!' he agreed philosophically.

There was no further communication from Simon Wetherby by the following morning, although Dolly had supplied him with her temporary address, and Makeda had almost forgotten about him by the time she set out for the offices of Messrs Gothram, Tynedall and Pettigrew for the second time.

Taking the bus to the junction of Broad Street and Shepherd, she walked the remaining distance to the familiar office block where she was told that Mr Pettigrew had not yet returned from lunch.

'He's had a rather busy morning,' the clerk in the outer office mentioned, 'but he's expecting you, Miss Garland. Will you go in and wait?'

Makeda prowled around the inner office, acknowledging her restlessness as the minutes ticked away, wondering what had kept James Pettigrew so long over what he generally described as 'a quick snack at the nearest tavern'. The papers he had been busy with during the morning lay undisturbed on the massive desk in the centre of the room, but they were mostly letters and files. There was no sign of her father's precious notes anywhere and her heart sank with disappointment. Perhaps the London solicitors had found nothing of importance to send.

A movement behind her made her turn. Grant Ogilvie was standing in the doorway between the two offices.

'Ah, Sheba!' he said as if they had parted on the best of terms. 'Am I interrupting something?'

'I'm waiting for Mr Pettigrew,' she told him. 'How did you manage to get past the outside office?'

'Without encountering the Dragon in mortal combat, do you mean?' He laughed abruptly. 'I stole a march on her and came up by the back stairs, but I had no idea you would still be waiting. James didn't mention it over lunch. We had a beer and a sandwich at the Club before we went to inspect some property I'm interested in.'

He had told her that he was in Bridgetown on business and it was sheer coincidence that their lawyers should be the same, yet she considered him with open hostility when she said:

'My appointment was for three o'clock. I'm surprised Mr Pettigrew forgot about it.'

'You're anxious about your father's notes,' he suggested, coming to stand beside her. 'I wouldn't worry, if I were you. He wasn't the sort of man who would lose things of great importance to him. Neither was my uncle, but we could have some sorting out to do. I take it you have no other source of information apart from the notes.'

She felt that it was time to tell him about Simon Wetherby.

'Something else has turned up,' she told him. 'A colleague of your uncle and my father wrote to my mother a week ago offering his help and we expect him to go back to Millo with us if he arrives here before we leave on the trader.'

His dark brows shot up in frank surprise.

'Millo is going to be a hive of industry,' he reflected. 'How long is it going to take you to complete the MS?'

When they spoke about the work she was doing she appeared to command his respect, but the remark about Millo flicked her on the raw.

'I've no idea how long it's going to take, especially when I have so little to go on with at present. We're—indebted to you for honouring your uncle's promise, of course, but if you want me to leave immediately, I'll go.'

Her challenge hung in the air between them for a full minute before he said coolly:

'Succoth doesn't interest me at present. You're welcome to the use of the house, Makeda, as I've just explained to James Pettigrew, but I intend to build on Millo. Otherwise, it would be on the market again. You needn't worry about "ugly little boxes" strewn all over the landscape, however. What I have in mind is bigger than that, but for the present you'll be safe enough at Succoth, even though it's falling down about your ears.'

It was painfully true. Succoth had been sadly in need of repair for a very long time, but its needs had come secondary to her father's research and it had appeared to hold together well enough. Rain came in on certain parts of the roof, but it rained so seldom on Millo that it hardly seemed to matter. What was important was the fact that the whole island was about to suffer change, and all because one man believed it necessary.

'You own so much,' she accused him angrily. 'Why couldn't you leave Millo alone?'

'Because I'm a man of business, as you constantly remind me,' he answered, his mouth clamping into a hard line. 'I don't believe in allowing anything to run to seed. Succoth you may use until you have no longer any need for it, but I reserve my right to do as I please with the rest of the island. Your mother sees my point of view, by the way, and she's not averse to company on Millo.'

'She intends to leave Succoth as soon as possible,' Makeda said heavily, unable to keep a note of bitterness out of her voice. 'She's never been really happy on the island; she has always felt "trapped", shut up alone with her children when her husband was abroad and frankly bored with his work when he came home to Succoth to write about it. Oh, I know what you're going to say,' she added before he could speak. 'She had a right to her own form of happiness, and I appreciate that, but my father's work was his life and he did take her everywhere with him in the beginning.' Her voice shook. 'He loved her, and he sold Millo to give her the freedom she always wanted.'

'What about your brother?' Grant asked, dismissing Dolly without comment.

'Heber? He has never felt as I do about Millo. Perhaps he's inherited Father's wanderlust.' She used the word for want of a better one. 'But he has another year to do at college before he qualifies. After that——'

She hesitated, while he waited for her to continue.

'After that,' she concluded on a quivering breath, 'our family will break up.'

'Thanks to me? Would it help if I offered you Succoth as a permanent home?' asked Grant.

She gazed at him incredulously.

'Why?' she demanded suspiciously. 'You must have some reason,' she declared when he did not answer her immediately. 'You would never make a concession like that unless it suited you, unless there was some personal gain attached to the bargain.'

He turned on his heel, leaving her beside the desk.

'How well you appear to know me,' he laughed. 'It would

suit me more than a little to keep Millo inhabited until I'm ready to build there.'

She stood in the slanting rays of sunlight pouring in at the window behind her, feeling chilled in spite of the re-flected warmth.

'You make no bones about it!' she cried. 'We would be a convenience to you until you were able to see us off the premises for good. No, Mr Ogilvie, as soon as my father's MS is completed, I'll go!'

'And you don't want my uncle's notes? Your pride wouldn't allow you to use them, I suppose.'

'They're your property,' she said. 'I couldn't possibly use them.'

'Not even though they held the secret of Sheba's gems?' He was laughing at her now. 'You surprise me, Makeda. I thought you more worthy than that, more dedicated to your father's memory. I would admire your spirit if you were not so completely irrational,' he added, pausing in the doorway. 'Remind me about my uncle's notes if you ever have need of them.'

He strode through the outer office, leaving her beside the desk with her heart hammering against her ribs and her eyes full of angry tears. How could she remain at Succoth while he came to the island to change it out of all recognition?

It was another five minutes before James Pettigrew re-turned full of apologies for having kept her waiting.

'I've ordered some tea to be sent in,' he announced. 'It's an old English custom that dies hard out here!'

'Mr Pettigrew,' she asked, 'have you got my father's notes?'

'They're here.' He unlocked a drawer in his desk. 'Quite a sheaf of them, as a matter of fact. I've made them up into a tidy parcel for you,' he added, pushing a large manilla en-velope towards her. 'They should keep you busy for some considerable time.'

She lifted the envelope to examine it closely, but there was nothing on the outside but her own name neatly typed on a white label. There could be a letter inside, though;

some message or other from her father which she could hardly wait to read.

It was several minutes before their tea was brought in and they discussed Millo while they waited. James Pettigrew had known the island for a long time and he had drawn up the contract for the sale of the existing lease.

'I wouldn't worry too much about it changing hands again,' he assured her. 'I'm quite impressed by the professor's nephew, as a matter of fact. He's a young man after my own heart and it's really very generous of him to let you stay on at Succoth until you are ready to go.'

'I suppose he can afford that sort of gesture.' Makeda sipped her tea. 'He knows we won't outstay our welcome. As soon as I can hand over the completed MS to Andresson and Marks, I'll go.'

They spoke about her father's book and then about London before the clerk came in to announce his next appointment.

'I have a Mr Ogilvie waiting,' the woman announced. 'He was here shortly after three o'clock with the information you wanted about the land, but decided to come back later. I must say, Mr Pettigrew, that I object to clients using the back entrance,' she went on to complain. 'One never really knows who's in and who's out, and with all these burglaries going on I think the door should be kept locked, even while we're here.'

James Pettigrew gave her a thoughtful smile.

'I can't think how he managed to evade you, Miss Mullony,' he murmured. 'But you caught him on the way out, I take it?'

'He had the grace to announce himself when he found that you weren't here. Shall I ask him to wait?'

'You can show him in.' James Pettigrew rose to his feet. 'It's time you two got to know each other, Makeda,' he declared. 'You may be going to see quite a lot of each other in the near future.'

'We've already met.' Makeda had jumped to her feet at the first mention of Grant Ogilvie's name. 'We didn't get on very well together,' she confessed, 'so I really must go.'

The sudden panic in her heart was inexplicable; she did not want to meet Grant Ogilvie again quite so soon.

Automatically she reached for the capacious sac which she had put on the floor beside her chair and rushed through the outer office with a brief nod of recognition which seemed to amuse Grant more than a little. He had become very friendly with her lawyer in a very short space of time, she decided.

Although the saner part of her mind demanded 'why the panic?' she was still hurrying by the time she reached the bus station, and it was only then that she remembered her father's notes. In her irrational flight from Grant Ogilvie she had left the precious parcel on Mr Pettigrew's desk !

It took her twenty minutes to hurry back across Trafalgar Square because the preparations for the final night of the carnival were in full swing and seemingly half of Barbados had come to watch. The ceremony of Burning Mr Harding would end Crop Over, with the effigy symbolising the ruthless gang-driver carted through the main street in a procession of decorated floats to his fatal end at the stake. It would all be very gay and very exciting, with fireworks, and singing, and dancing, but she had no time to think about carnival at the present moment.

The Dragon didn't seem greatly surprised to see her.

'You left your parcel,' she said, getting up from behind her typewriter. 'I noticed it as soon as you'd gone.'

Makeda heaved a sigh of relief. Through the opaque glass of the inner office door she could see the outline of two figures—Mr Pettigrew and Grant Ogilvie, she supposed—but there was no need to announce her presence if the Dragon had salvaged the notes.

'Mr Ogilvie rushed after you with the parcel, but you've obviously missed each other in the crowd.'

'You mean he has my father's papers?' Makeda gazed at her incredulously. 'Surely Mr Pettigrew knew that I would come back when I discovered I'd left them on his desk?'

'It was Mr Ogilvie's idea to go after you.' The older woman drew herself up to her full, commanding height. 'Mr Pettigrew had another client waiting.' She glanced towards the inner sanctum. 'He's in with him now.'

'Did—Mr Ogilvie say where he was going?' Makeda asked desperately.

The woman shrugged.

'We had no time to ask him. He rushed out as quickly as you did, but I think he said something about knowing your address if he didn't catch up with you.'

Makeda took a taxi back to St James'. It was a luxury she could ill afford, but she was far too worried about the fate of her precious parcel to wait for the next bus out. Another taxi was standing at the hotel door, but Grant Ogilvie was nowhere to be seen.

Heber and her mother were crossing the hall when she went in and she noticed automatically that her mother had changed into one of her more glamorous outfits.

'We're going to Seawell to meet Mr Wetherby,' she explained the waiting taxi. 'He's arriving on the next flight. We had a cable from him just after you left.'

'Oh——? Well, I won't stop you.' Makeda had other things on her mind. 'Will you bring him back here?' she enquired automatically.

'I've arranged everything with Mrs Burgess if he hasn't already made a reservation,' Dolly explained, pulling on a pair of white gloves.

'Be seeing you!' Heber grinned as he climbed into the taxi behind his mother.

Makeda paid off her own hire-car and went into the hotel to wait, but it was almost an hour later before Grant Ogilvie put in an appearance, the parcel containing her father's papers under his arm.

'You left these in the office when you dashed out in such a hurry,' he said. 'I knew you would be in a panic as soon as you realised you'd forgotten to pick them up, so I came after you. I was quite certain I would be able to overtake you within a block or two. You must be very fleet of foot, Sheba, or were you just running away?'

For the first time his mockery was lost on her.

'I went back to the office for them,' she explained, hugging the precious parcel to her breast, 'but the crowd was pretty thick around the Square. We must have passed each other without noticing.'

'That could happen,' he agreed. 'I went back to the office when I didn't find you at the bus stop, but you'd been and gone again. It was quite a paper-chase!'

'I'm very grateful,' she said, still clutching the envelope to her as if she couldn't quite believe that it was finally in her possession. 'Will you have something to drink? You must feel warm after all that rushing around.'

He followed her through to the patio where she rang for the waiter who was generally on duty by six o'clock.

'I'll have something long and thirst-quenching,' Grant decided. 'A lime punch, I think.'

'Two lime punches, Sam.' Makeda gave her order when the waiter appeared at the glass doors leading into the house. 'Large ones, with plenty of ice.' She sat down on the edge of a chair.

'Your mother has found quite a home from home,' Grant observed, wandering around the confined space while they waited for Sam to bring their drinks. 'She comes here quite often, I expect.'

'Whenever she's in Bridgetown.' Makeda was suddenly very much aware of his keen scrutiny as she laid the envelope on the table between them. 'It's comfortable without being too expensive. We've been coming to Waldon's for years.'

'But you would rather be on Millo.'

'A thousand times rather!' she agreed without thinking. 'There's no comparison.' Suddenly she was looking straight into his eyes, expressing her gratitude without reserve. 'I'll be there for the next few months, thanks to you. It means a great deal to me,' she confessed.

He walked round the overgrown flamboyant.

'Don't make it difficult for me, Sheba,' he said when he finally came to stand beside her. 'I think I prefer to do battle with you rather than see you humble yourself by trying to thank me for something anyone would have done in the circumstances.'

She looked away from his indifferent smile, determined not to argue with him this time because she really was grateful.

When their drinks came he sat down on one of the loungers, stretching his long legs out on it as if he meant to stay.

'We're expecting Simon Wetherby any minute,' she informed him.

He smiled at the too-broad hint, draining his glass slowly.

'Since I'll probably be introduced to him eventually on Millo, why not now?' he suggested to her immediate dismay. 'Does your mother know him?'

She shook her head.

'He couldn't have been with the expedition very long or we would have heard more about him. He was a new boy, straight from college, I think.'

A taxi crunched to a standstill outside the front door.

'That must be Mr Wetherby now,' Grant observed, getting to his feet. 'Do we rush to greet him?'

Makeda held her breath.

'Why should we?' she said, at last. 'He's Mother's cup of tea. After all, she invited him.'

Dolly came out to the patio, introducing her protégé with a flourish.

'This is Simon,' she said. 'I'm sure we're all going to get on very well together. Oh,' she exclaimed, noticing their other guest, 'we're quite a party, aren't we? You'll stay, of course? We'll have something to eat together.'

Makeda introduced them, aware of Simon Wetherby looking closely at her. He was a personable young man with piercing blue eyes and fair hair which he parted in the middle, and when he shook her hand he held it much longer than he should have done.

'I've been looking forward to meeting you for a very long time,' he told her, 'ever since I first heard your name! It was positively inspired, and I suppose it was your father's idea. Or was it your mother's?' He turned to beam at Dolly.

'You can't imagine how much all this means to me, Mrs Garland, meeting you at last.'

Dolly turned to Grant.

'We'll run across each other on Millo, I suppose, while Makeda is finishing John's book,' she said.

'That's possible,' Grant returned, waiting to be introduced to Simon.

The two men shook hands, measuring each other with a speculative glance. They were as different as they could possibly be, Makeda thought, and they were not going to like each other.

From the moment he arrived at Waldon's Simon Wetherby was a force to be reckoned with. Apart from being so physically attractive, he had a charming manner which contrasted with Grant's rather grim approach to the situation when they discussed Millo.

'I can't wait to get there,' he announced at the dinner table when Jacinthe had finally joined them and Mrs Burgess had graciously agreed to the trouble of an extra guest. 'It's been described to me so often and so vividly by the Professor that I seem to know every nook and cranny. I don't think the Lesser Antilles have been explored to their full extent,' he went on soberly. 'I'd like to get right down to the Arawaks and work back from there. They were a fascinating race, you know, with their own culture, in spite of the fact that we tend to class them as savages nowadays. My theory is that they mined a great deal of precious metal for their everyday use and their source is still to be discovered. It's an individual belief, of course, but fascinating to think about.'

'You won't find much to occupy you on Millo,' Grant remarked dryly. 'The original inhabitants were Carib Indians who were virtually nomads, and the island has been thoroughly surveyed in the past few years. If you're interested in local legend, however,' he added with an oblique glance in Makeda's direction, 'we're apparently rich in it. Our culture isn't very old, but we have the odd ruin or two to keep us busy.'

'Fascinating!' Simon agreed with a pleasant smile. 'To get

69

back to the present, though, do you intend to work on the island?' he asked.

'Eventually,' Grant told him. 'I'm in no great hurry.'

'I knew your uncle very well.' Simon toyed with the sweet the waitress had placed before him, an elaborate concoction of tropical fruits piled high in a tall glass with a froth of whipped cream on top. 'We worked together for over a year. He had several theories about the Saudi Arabian mines, quite apart from the recent finds there, and I'm sure he must have written most of them down.'

He paused, but Grant refused to rise to the obvious bait.

'I haven't had time to go through my uncle's papers in great detail,' he said evenly. 'He made copious notes, of course, but it will take some time to sort them out.'

Dolly turned the conversation away from Millo and Saudi Arabia to remark that they would be missing the final day of the Festival by returning with the trader the following afternoon.

'Simon ought to see the Burning of Mr Harding,' she smiled. 'Mr Harding was a wicked gang-driver in the bad old days of the Sugar Barons, Simon,' she explained, 'and the Bajans burn his effigy on the final night of carnival. There are all sorts of excitements in Bridgetown and along the coast. It really is a pity that we have to go.'

'I'll be taking *Seafarer* down to Grenada on Sunday.' Grant made the offer so impatiently. 'I could drop you off at Millo on the way.'

Oh, Mother! Makeda protested inwardly. Why do you have to be so obvious!

'That would be wonderful!' Dolly enthused. 'But is there really room for us all?'

'On a day trip, yes. We managed very well on the way across,' Grant told her.

'Abi won't be going back, so we're really only one extra,' Dolly calculated. 'I have to warn you, though, I have an awful lot of luggage.'

'I think we ought to go by the trader, as we arranged,'

Makeda broke in. 'After all, Millo isn't on the direct route to Grenada.'

'Grant won't mind,' said Heber. 'An hour or two is neither here nor there at sea, you know, and I'd be more than willing to offer my services in the wheelhouse!'

Seafarer had captured his fancy on their journey to Barbados and Grant and he had become friends. Makeda tried not to see it as a betrayal on her brother's part, reasoning that Heber spent most of his time away from the island and probably didn't think about Millo in such emotional terms as she did.

Grant looked questioningly at Dolly, who had never been averse to an extra day or two in a 'civilised atmosphere'.

'It would be much more comfortable than going with the trader,' she agreed. 'You really are very kind, Mr Ogilvie, though I can't think why.' She treated him to one of her dazzling smiles. 'I'm sure nobody is going to object to such a trip in this wonderful weather.'

Except Makeda, Grant's quizzical glance seemed to say as they rose from the table to take their coffee out in the soft darkness of the patio.

It was eleven o'clock before he finally rose to go, having settled himself comfortably into one of the cane loungers to listen to Simon with half-closed eyes and a faintly amused smile on his lips.

'Tomorrow,' Simon said, 'someone must show me Barbados. You, Makeda?' he asked pointedly when Abi explained that she would be flying out to New York on an early flight.

Makeda hesitated.

'Heber knows far more about Barbados than I do,' she hedged. 'I'd rather like to start work on my father's notes.'

'Really, Makeda!' Dolly protested, 'you're taking this book far too seriously. There may be nothing of interest in the papers you've just received.'

Simon was standing close behind her.

'Forgive me, Mrs Garland,' he said quickly, 'I think there must be. They were very securely guarded, both by your husband and Professor Hunt.' He looked across the patio at Grant. 'They kept individual records, but I think your husband's were the most precise.'

Grant kept his own counsel about the nature of his uncle's notes, if he knew it. He was standing in the shadow of the giant flamboyant and even when he emerged from it to say goodnight his face was inscrutable. As he passed Makeda he said lightly:

'Don't forget the mounted police and the good old Nelson tradition, and there's always the Scotland district to blow Mr Wetherby's cobwebs away.'

But Makeda could not take Simon on a sightseeing tour of the east coast. To return to Bathsheba and motor along the spectacular road to Andromeda or northwards to Cattlewash would only renew her memories of the journey they had made to St Joseph and the careless little kiss Grant had placed on her brow.

Her heart was a tumult of emotion as she recalled the intimacy of the meal they had shared and how wrongly it had turned out in the end because they had argued, once again, about Millo.

Simon proved the easiest of companions. Since Heber had decided to spend the following day with Grant victualling *Seafarer* and Jacinthe and Dolly went to Seawell to see Abi off to New York, it was left to Makeda to entertain their guest. She did her best, hiring an open landau to take them on a tour of the Careenage where the trading schooners lay and right round the Bay to the Garrison and up to Rendezvous Hill. They had lunch at Silver Sands on the south coast, deciding, by mutual consent, that the afternoon was too warm for any more sightseeing.

'Let's just laze and talk,' Simon suggested. 'I've eaten far too big a lunch even to walk!'

'We could go back to Sandy Lane and bathe,' Makeda suggested, thus avoiding any suggestion of a trip to the east coast later in the afternoon. 'Whatever you would like.'

'It's what *you* would like,' he said, moving nearer. 'Makeda, I seem to have known you for a very long time.'

'Not quite twenty-four hours,' she reminded him.

He put a firm hand over hers.

'Hours mean very little in working out a friendship,' he declared.

When she moved her hand away, he laughed.

'I wish I'd met a girl like you years ago,' he said with absolute sincerity.

'You must have met dozens of girls in your time,' Makeda countered. 'Girls who are far more intelligent than I am.'

'That's exactly my point.' He captured her hand again to pull her to her feet. 'I don't like ultra-intelligent females who thrust their superiority at me from the word "go". I prefer my women sweet and pliable.'

'With no will of their own,' Makeda suggested, leading the way on to the beach. 'That won't do, Simon, in this day and age.'

'You've got me all wrong,' he tried to convince her. 'I'm not averse to a dash of spirit or even a hint of wilfulness which might add spice to a situation, but the Militant Woman makes me want to run for shelter like a frightened rabbit!'

'I could never think of you as a rabbit,' she laughed because he amused her so much. 'A dog, perhaps. A very gay dog!'

'Now you're being cruel and I'm mortally offended!' He pulled her down on to the soft white sand. 'Tell me about Millo,' he demanded, lying back with his head cradled in his clasped hands.

'You must wait and decide for yourself,' she told him because, somehow, she did not want to talk about Millo now.

'All right, I will,' he agreed. 'Your mother has been so generous about all this that I can't quite believe it. I've thought about Millo so often as the place where your father did his real work. When you're out on a dig it's so hot and dusty and there's all the day-by-day concentration of getting somewhere and the excitement of the next find, and then it all has to be written down and brought back to somewhere like Millo to be presented in its true perspective. One has to get right away from a subject to assess it properly in one's own time.'

'My father had very little time,' Makeda said quietly. 'He was only half-way through his notes when he had to leave again. He was a slow worker, a "dear muddler", we used to say.'

She was able to talk to Simon because he understood about her father's work, and no doubt Professor Hunt had also trusted him. It was only Grant who seemed dubious about him, suspecting his motives, perhaps, but Grant was the sort of person who would want to probe to the very roots of a situation before he accepted anyone. Trust and friendship at first sight was not exactly his cup of tea, and perhaps that was why he had been so successful in business. Her own madly impulsive nature could have done nothing to endear her to him.

Simon's hair was almost the colour of the sand, she reflected, aware of the keen blue eyes watching her from under his half-closed lids, and in a good many ways he was an enigma to her, too. He had stormed his way into her life, stirring up the backwater of her quiet existence, seemingly determined to make her accept him and the help he had to offer.

Did she want this? Lazily she thrust the pertinent question aside to be answered at some other time, probably when she was alone.

They swam for an hour in the warm, turquoise water with the heat of the sun full on their backs and the gentle undulation of the tide lapping over them when they floated, face upwards, to talk. A strong swimmer from her earliest days, Makeda found her match in Simon, who seemed equally tireless, and when they finally waded ashore he laughed.

'You're so like a mermaid I wouldn't be surprised if you ran back into the sea and disappeared,' he declared, putting a damp arm round her waist as he shook back his fair hair to dry it in the sun. 'Are you a mermaid, Makeda, escaped from "sand-strewn caverns, cool and deep"? You look suspiciously like one now with your wet hair hanging down your back and those sea-green eyes!'

'No!' she objected sharply because Grant Ogilvie had teased her in much the same way. 'My eyes aren't green at all. They're mostly blue.'

'With all sorts of tawny lights in them, like flakes of sunshine on green water! Don't underestimate yourself, Makeda, even if you do live on a remote island away from anywhere,' he cautioned, leaning purposefully towards her, his own eyes full of admiration.

She pushed him away before he could attempt to kiss her.

'Time to go!' she announced. 'It's dangerous to lie too long in the sun.'

'Not here, in such an amazing paradise,' he protested. 'It can't be much more than three o'clock.'

'It's after four, and we have to find our way back to St James before dark,' she reminded him. 'We promised to take Jacinthe on the town, remember?'

He picked up her towelling shift from the sand.

'Who taught you to play hard-to-get?' he demanded.

She pulled the shift over her head.

'I wasn't playing, Simon,' she said. 'I—just don't want us to start off on the wrong foot. I don't like compliments, you see, unless they're sincerely meant.'

He took her by the shoulders, looking into her eyes.

'And you don't think mine were for true?' he asked. 'How wrong you are, Makeda! This isn't a flash-in-the-pan or a first-sight infatuation. I've known you longer than you think. Your father used to talk about you a great deal when we were alone, and what he told me made me all the more eager to meet you. In some ways,' he added slowly, 'I suppose he treated me like a son.'

She was instantly ashamed.

'Oh, Simon, I didn't mean to be rude!' she apologised. 'I'm just—not the kissing kind. Not on first acquaintance, anyway. I would have to feel that you meant something to me, that we really did have an awful lot in common——'

Her explanation drifted away into the shadow of the

palms and a chill little wind seemed to stir along the beach. It was time to go.

Jacinthe was waiting for them when they got back to the hotel.

'Aunt Dolly has gone to lie down for an hour,' she announced. 'She's completely exhausted by her day in Bridgetown, and so am I.'

'You belie the fact!' Simon told her with one of his brilliant smiles. 'You can't wait to join the revelry. Where can we eat, after you've left a message for your mother?'

'There are dozens of restaurants,' Makeda told him, 'but I can't go like this. Give me half an hour to get washed and changed.'

'You'll have to do something about your hair,' Jacinthe advised. 'It's all tacky with salt water.'

Makeda washed her hair under the shower, giving it a quick blow-dry with Jacinthe's dryer, and scrambled into the green cotton dress which had been pressed for her by one of the maids. She looked reasonably presentable, she thought, as she hurried quickly down the stairs to where Simon and Jacinthe were waiting.

Simon had changed into light trousers and a blue shirt with a darker blue cravat knotted fashionably at his throat, and his skin looked pleasantly tanned.

'I expect I'll need this,' he remarked, picking up a navy blue blazer from one of the sitting-room chairs. 'Have we any idea where we're going?'

'We'll have to take our chance,' Makeda said. 'Everywhere will be packed solid.'

'Should we try somewhere apart from Bridgetown?' he asked.

'No, I think we should stay fairly near at hand. We haven't got our own transport and a hire-car will cost the earth if we keep it waiting outside a country restaurant for more than an hour.'

Makeda knew that she was making an excuse because she didn't want to return to the rugged east coast where she had gone with Grant in case, by the merest coincidence, they should meet again.

'Just as you say,' Simon agreed. 'One restaurant is as good as another as far as I'm concerned since I don't know Bridgetown at all.'

He phoned for a taxi while Makeda went up to her mother's bedroom. Dolly had made no effort to change and was asleep on a chaise-longue in the darkened room, her feet blissfully bare, her abandoned sandals lying on the floor where she had dropped them. The room itself was in hopeless disarray, as if she had made a search for something on her return, and the parcels she had brought back with her from the shops were scattered on every available chair.

'Mother!' Makeda whispered, but there was no response. Evidently Dolly would sleep away her exhaustion until Heber returned in time for dinner with her.

She scribbled a note, quite sure that her mother would not want to accompany them back into 'the fray', as she called Bridgetown when it suited her.

'All ready?' Simon asked when she rejoined him in the hall. 'Jacinthe suggests we try the Net & Trident or the Peebles if we want to keep in the city. It'll be noisy, of course, but fun.'

They piled into the taxi when it arrived, Jacinthe sitting on one of the folding seats with her back to the driver, while Simon sat too close to Makeda opposite. Mammy's lace shawl lay on the seat beside Makeda and she thrust it between them.

'Hi, that looks beautiful,' Simon remarked. 'It's handworked, of course.'

'Our housekeeper knitted it for me.' Somehow, the lovely, fine shawl seemed too precious a thing to discuss with a stranger.

'Mammy?' Simon asked. 'She's someone else I have to meet. Your father depended upon her quite a lot.'

It was a statement rather than a direct question and Makeda made no reply, but Jacinthe said:

'Mammy practically brought us up when everybody else

was away. Mammy and Ben were always there and we came to depend on them. You'll like them, Simon, I'm sure.'

Jacinthe, who was normally so quiet, was basking in the warmth of Simon's outgoing personality, flattered by his apparent approval and ready to laugh at any small joke he made as Heber and Dolly had done from the moment they had met. He was gay and amusing, Makeda allowed, and the right companion for the final days of carnival.

Bridgetown was so crowded with revellers that they had to try several restaurants before they found one with a table to spare, and it was several minutes before Makeda realised that they were being watched. When she turned her head she found herself looking straight into Grant Ogilvie's critical eyes.

He was seated on the far side of the tiny dance-floor, sharing a table with the most beautiful girl she had ever seen.

Grant treated her to a coolly impartial bow while his companion turned her head to look, half-smiling as she followed his gaze across the dance floor.

'How could anyone be so beautiful?' said Jacinthe. 'She's like a lily, isn't she, all white and gold and untouchable.'

'You amaze me!' Simon laughed. 'But you've rather hit the nail on the head this time. Save me from the cool celestial type, though,' he grinned. 'I'd rather have a tiger-lily any day.'

'You're not being asked,' Makeda retorted. 'She's Grant Ogilvie's exclusive property, judging by the way they're looking at each other.'

All through the leisurely-served meal and the gay little cabaret which followed she was acutely aware of the couple at the other table, although Grant made no effort to acknowledge them after that one brief nod of recognition. The two seemed to be shut into a world of their own, deep in conversation and oblivious to anything else though several heads turned in their direction when they took the floor for one solitary dance. Even the compelling music of limbo seemed to pass them by, they had so much to say to each other, although they did turn in the dancers' direction out of courtesy from time to time.

It was after midnight before they rose to go, and Makeda, Jacinthe and Simon followed them out, but their cab was pulling away from the swing doors before they reached them. Makeda had a last, fleeting glimpse of the girl in the light of a flare as the cab turned into Prince William Henry Street and disappeared from view.

'Ogilvie certainly likes his women tall and sleek,' Simon observed. 'I wonder who she is.'

'Someone important, I've no doubt,' Makeda answered sharply, 'but we're not going to find a cab if we stand here speculating all night!'

Simon smiled at the quick flash of temper which had deepened the green in her eyes.

'Leave it to your Uncle Simon,' he said. 'I've got a way with taxi-drivers.' He flagged one down. 'What did I tell you? They come to me like moths to a candle on a dark night!'

The streets were still crowded and their progress was slow. Makeda sat on the edge of her seat, gazing out at the smiling faces of the revellers without seeming to see them. The colourful scene was like a gay kaleidoscope which had suddenly blurred and which, when shaken again, could so easily change into a different pattern, as her beloved island would be changed if Grant Ogilvie brought his lovely companion with him to Millo.

She had been looking forward to their return to the island aboard *Seafarer*, but now she was wishing with all her heart that she had gone home with the trader as she had intended to do.

CHAPTER FOUR

The morning after the final scene of carnival was always something of an anti-climax, but they had little time to dwell on the fact as they prepared to join *Seafarer* for the journey to Millo.

Heber had returned to the hotel the evening before, having spent most of the afternoon on the ketch helping Grant, but he made no reference to any extra passenger. The Beautiful Lady, as Simon persisted in calling Grant's companion, didn't appear to be coming with them.

Nor was she at the Yacht Club to see them depart. Grant was completely businesslike, welcoming them aboard as he called his instructions to Heber, and only when Makeda nearly missed her footing as she jumped foolhardily from the wharf did he single her out for his undivided attention.

'Careful, Sheba!' he cautioned, his fingers fastening hard on her bare arm. 'We're hardly equipped for a catastrophe before we sail!'

She had scraped her leg rather badly against the gunwale as she landed, but she would not let him inspect the damage.

'I'm not mortally wounded,' she declared. 'Don't make a fuss!'

They sailed out across Carlisle Bay with the sun glittering on the white buildings behind them and on the incredibly blue water ahead. *Seafarer* took to the deep like the thoroughbred she was, dipping gracefully before each wave as they came to meet her, her sails filling as the gentle trade wind bore her along.

Even before they had left port Dolly had decided to spend the voyage below decks, ensconcing herself in the day cabin with her feet up and every comfort which Grant could devise close at hand. She had decided to write her bread-and-butter letters straight away, but when Makeda went below after the first hour out she was fast asleep.

When she went up on deck again she found the others gathered in the wheelhouse and she made her way farther aft to sit in the sun. Presently Grant came to stand above her, one hand on the mast, his long legs straddled out on the roof of the after-cabin, his grey eyes ranging to the far horizon's rim.

'You should be home by six o'clock,' he informed her. 'Before dark, anyway.'

The word 'home' had pierced straight to her heart, but she could not let him see the effect it had on her.

'What are you going to do?' she asked. 'Are you going on to Grenada immediately?'

He considered the question as if he hadn't given it a great deal of thought.

'I needn't, as a matter of fact,' he said. 'I could easily spend the night aboard in Frenchman's Cove.'

It was a direct challenge and he waited for her response, but she was in no mood to argue with him at that moment.

'Is Wetherby going to stay for long?' he asked.

'I'm not sure.' She met his eyes in the bright sunlight. 'He wants to help with the book.'

'What do *you* want?' he asked almost casually. 'If I remember rightly, you once told me that your father's papers were too precious to be shared with a stranger. Have they suddenly become less personal, or are you completely convinced of Wetherby's sincerity?'

She narrowed her eyes against the sun.

'Shouldn't I be?' she demanded sharply. 'What do you feel about him?'

'Nothing, at the moment. I don't believe in first impressions, Sheba, although you seem to go in for them in a big way.'

'Simon's absolutely charming,' Makeda protested because she knew that he was never really serious when he called her 'Sheba'. 'Everyone likes him.'

'Including Heber and your mother,' he mused. 'I must be mistaken, in that case. Charming people tend to put me on my guard until I know them better, but I could be so wrong this time.'

'And you don't like to be wrong,' she shot at him. 'You calculate every little move before you make it so that nobody can trip you up or—or make a fool of you!'

'That's a fair enough assessment,' he agreed. 'Once I made a grave error of judgement by being too impetuous, Sheba, and I paid for it for a very long time afterwards. It made me determined to think very carefully before I committed myself in the future. Did you enjoy your dinner on Friday?' he asked abruptly. 'I thought you looked less than happy when you first came in.'

'We had trouble getting a table. We'd tried several places,' she explained. 'I suppose we should have booked beforehand, but it was a sort of impulsive thing, in the end.'

'Simon will know better next time.' He glanced at his watch. 'What I really came to ask was will you have a look at things in the galley. I brought what I thought we would need aboard early this morning, but if there isn't enough you can always raid the stores.'

'I wouldn't like to leave you on short tack after we'd gone,' she said quickly.

'I'm only going as far as Grenada,' he reminded her. 'After that I'll be coming to Millo to take a closer look at my inheritance.'

She had to swallow a hardness in her throat before she could say casually:

'We could let you have milk and eggs, and Mammy bakes fresh bread-cake every day.'

'You make me feel that I shall have to come,' he said, turning along the deck.

Who will you bring to Millo with you? The Beautiful Lady, perhaps, if she's flown from Seawell to Grenada in the meantime?

The question plagued her for the remainder of the short voyage. They came to Millo as the sun went down, flaunting its vermilion and gold banners above the sea and staining all the sky with their reflected light. Grant steered *Seafarer* into Frenchman's Cove.

'You'll come up to the house for something to eat?' Dolly invited. 'It's been so kind of you to bring us back.'

Grant hesitated. It was just light enough to see Mammy and her family standing on the verandah steps shading their eyes against the afterglow as they watched *Seafarer's* progress, and suddenly Makeda's heart began to beat faster as they came nearer to the only place she had ever been able to call home. Beyond the coconut palms which fringed the shore and backed by the darker scrub, Succoth lay half hidden in the clearing which had once been a delightful tropical garden. Its low, thatched roof seemed to hold all the latent warmth of the day and the stonework glowed with the colour of the aftermath as it faded from flamboyant vermilion through a deep rose to a soft apricot pink.

'It's very kind of you,' Grant was saying as he took up her mother's invitation. 'I've heard a great deal about Mammy's cooking,' he added, looking in Makeda's direction for a moment before he went forward to drop the anchor while Heber coped with the sails.

Jacinthe was at the wheel, her piquant little face flushed with endeavour as she strove to prove how efficient she was, and for the first time Makeda saw her, not as a child, but as an intelligent young woman who might appeal to any man. She had appeared shy and ill at ease in Grant's company at first, but now she had blossomed in a quiet way which made her look almost beautiful. Her eyes, softly caressing, rested on the thatched roof of Succoth as Makeda's had done and she still held *Seafarer's* wheel after the ketch had swung round into the wind to ride peacefully at anchor in the cove.

Grant strode along the deck to release the dinghy and Makeda saw his tall figure silhouetted against the glow of the western sky. They had come home to Succoth and he was with them, whether she liked it or not.

Mammy greeted them with her customary candour.

'Why you no' come with the trader?' she demanded, eyeing the two extra guests as they came up the beach with Jacinthe.

'It was much more convenient to come this way,' Dolly explained. 'It gave us an extra two days in Bridgetown. Mr Ogilvie will be staying to dinner and Mr Wetherby will be our guest for a week or two.'

It was the first time Makeda had heard a definite duration put on Simon's visit, but she supposed he had discussed it with her mother. Dolly, of course, would have to entertain him because she would be too busy with her father's notes. She meant to start work straight away.

Mammy's dark eyes were fixed steadily on the two strangers.

'Why they come?' she asked on a note of prophecy. 'They bring nothing but trouble to this island. Yo' mark ma words, Miss Garland. Yo' jus' mark ma words!'

'Oh, Mammy, you're impossible!' Dolly protested. 'They're both very nice young men.'

Mammy was looking at Makeda, who had turned to wait for the others.

'You come home to work, Miss Makeda,' she said. 'Yo' jus' see that yo' do. Two young men is one too many, if yo' ask me, an' there's one will do yo' no good if yo' trust him more than yo' ought.'

'Mammy! For goodness' sake stop predicting and get us something to eat!' Dolly exclaimed. 'We're ravenous.'

'The dinner be all ready an' waitin',' the Carib woman told her with dignity. 'Yo' an' yo' gusets have only to sit down an' eat it, Miss Garland.'

The meal, which had probably been ready since the trader was due, was excellent and Mammy served it with a good grace once she had unburdened herself of her frustration and and a certain amount of anxiety about their wellbeing when they had not returned in the normal way. She had shooed Ben and her numerous children back to their quarters, clearing the verandah where Ben had lit the lamps, and Dolly led her guests out into the velvet darkness to pour coffee for them under the stars.

When the others had eased themselves into the rickety cane loungers Grant remained standing, although he accepted a cup of coffee from Dolly as if he meant to stay. He looked about him as frankly as he had done in the dining-room, taking in the shabby paintwork and the broken downcomer which let the water cascade from the roof on to the steps when the rain came. He was adding it all up, Makeda thought with a catch in her throat, taking stock to see what kind of bargain he had made. Succoth would be his, too, now that he had come into his inheritance.

Moving into the shadows, she sat down on a canvas chair away from the table where her mother was holding court.

'Why so reserved, of a sudden?' Simon was standing over her. 'I've come to see if you want a refill.'

She looked down at her half-empty cup.

'I've had sufficient, thank you.' She drained the lukewarm drink under his watching eye. 'I'm not very keen on coffee.'

He looked beyond her into the shadows surrounding the house.

'Do you fancy a walk?' he asked. 'It's light enough to go down to the beach.'

Something restless within her prompted her to accept his invitation for what it was. Simon, the romantic, could not resist the starlight and the girl!

'You won't see much,' she warned. 'You should have left your first impression of Frenchman's till the morning.'

He took her arm as they went together down the steps, looking up through the ragged palm-fronds to the star-bright sky.

'This was the moment I wanted,' he assured her, 'ever since I heard your father describe the island. He was very fond of Millo and he planned to work here for a long time.'

'Please,' Makeda protested, 'don't let's talk about it. Sometimes it's very hard for me to believe that he's dead.'

'It must be,' he said. 'You worked so well together.'

They walked a little way in silence, coming eventually to

the beach where Makeda kicked off her shoes to go bare-footed on the sand.

'Your mother has asked me to stay,' Simon said.

'Then you will, I suppose.'

'If I can be any help to you, Makeda.'

She turned to look at him in the bright starlight.

'I don't know that I need help,' she answered. 'I'm half-way through the manuscript and those final notes won't take very long to sort out.' Her voice shook a little. 'Then it will all be finished and we shall leave Millo for ever.'

'Where will you go?'

'I don't know. I don't mean to think about it till the very last moment because I can't bear the thought of never seeing Millo again.'

'Your brother told me about the sale. Do you mean to ask Ogilvie to reconsider your tenancy?'

'How could I?' All the stormy protest of her loss lay in the dark pools of her eyes. 'I couldn't *ask* for Succoth, not from anyone like Grant. He would think it despicable after he'd agreed to honour his uncle's contract. He needn't have done that, you know. He could have turned us out immediately.'

'Maybe he has no need for Succoth,' he suggested. 'What does he intend to do with the island, anyway?'

'Build on it. He said so.'

'Hotels, do you mean?'

'He didn't go into details. He just said he was going to build, but what else would he want to put on Millo but a Holiday Inn or something equally repugnant?'

'I gather you don't like the idea at all,' he said slowly. 'How long have you got?'

'On Millo? Not very long.'

'Supposing we get together and spin the time out a bit,' he suggested. 'Would that help?'

'Not in the least, Simon. If I can't do anything else, I can play fair. Besides, the publishers are waiting.' Her lips firmed as she thought of her conversation with Grant when they had discussed his uncle's notes. 'My father's book must be first on the market.'

'Which brings you back to me.' He put his arm about her shoulders. 'You really do need my help, Makeda. We could do this together, and after the book is published you might even be able to buy Succoth, if you still wanted it.'

'It wouldn't be the same,' she told him emphatically, freeing herself from his encircling arm. 'It's not just Succoth,' she added bleakly. 'It's Millo and all it stands for. Succoth is just about falling down, but I love it. I've never wanted to live anywhere else, but if Millo was spoiled, if it was turned into a holiday resort, I couldn't live here remembering what it had been like.'

'Poor you!' Simon took her hand. 'I wish I was a millionaire and then I could buy you a dozen Millos!'

'Don't joke about it!' she cried sharply, aware that a dark figure had detached itself from the shadows of the coconut palms and was walking along the beach towards them.

Grant was on his way back to *Seafarer*, but she felt that he had been standing in the shadow of the palms longer than they realised.

'If you would like a sail across to Grenada in the morning,' he said when they came together, 'I'd be only to pleased to take you.'

Simon measured him with a wary eye.

'Thanks all the same,' he said, 'but I've promised myself some really energetic swimming. There's a lot to see on the island, I gather, and I'd like to help Makeda, if I can.'

Grant turned to look at Makeda, at last.

'I take it you enjoyed your trip to Barbados,' he said evenly.

'Yes. I haven't thanked you,' she acknowledged, 'but I do appreciate all you've done.'

How formal and insincere that sounded! Makeda turned away from his searching gaze, wondering why he had come down on to the beach to reach *Seafarer*. He could have gone direct from the house on to the jetty. His dinghy was moored to the rail where they had left it, and she watched him slip the painter and row out towards the ketch over the clear, dark water of the cove. He would leave *Seafarer* at anchor there during the night because it would be foolhardy to attempt the entrance to Green Turtle in the darkness, but when he returned from Grenada he would use the other bay. How foolish he must have thought her when she had told him in no uncertain manner that he was trespassing on an island which really belonged to him!

'He's the complete autocrat,' Simon observed, following the progress of the dinghy across the cove. 'I suppose you get like that when you have eveything, but his uncle was a very modest man, like your father.'

'They were completely immersed in their work. Perhaps it isn't a very good thing to be so—remote from everyday living,' Makeda reflected. 'Professor Hunt relegated everything else to his nephew.'

'Including the development business? Ah well, money tends to make money, and Ogilvie will go on building his empire in spite of us so good luck to him, I say!'

Simon turned from his contemplation of *Seafarer* to look up at the house where Dolly had left a single lamp burning on the verandah. There was a frown between his brows and his eyes were frankly calculating. He had come a long way to meet John Garland's daughter and he was determined not to be sidetracked by Grant Ogilvie or anyone else.

CHAPTER FIVE

In the morning, when Makeda looked out of her bedroom window, *Seafarer* had gone. Grant must have taken up the anchor and slipped away with the dawn wind, sailing out beyond the Dutchman's Cap towards Grenada before any of them were fully awake.

The cove looked curiously empty, although her own dinghy rocked gently at the jetty steps, and suddenly she decided to take it out and sail as far as she could before the wind dropped. She had been far too long in Barbados without being able to sail off into the blue on her own!

Only Mammy's children were about at such an early hour, together with the ubiquitous hens. The noise they made was all part of Millo, the part she would remember as long as she lived.

The children stood in a straggling line on the beach to watch her set out, but this morning she did not beckon to the oldest boy to join her. There was so much she had to think about and on Barbados she had hardly been able to think at all.

The light wind took her as far as the Dutchman's Cap, which she circumnavigated stretched out on the floorboards of the tiny well with her bare foot on the tiller and the sheet wound round her hand. She would have to drift back most of the way and be late for breakfast, but food and regulated mealtimes had never mattered at Succoth. A huge bowl of fruit was always kept available on the dining-room table, and there was an abundance of goat's milk to be had in the kitchen, together with the luscious, warm bread-cake which was Mammy's speciality.

Soon all that would be gone. Makeda's fingers tightened on

the sheet as she wondered what would happen to Mammy and Ben when they finally left Millo. Perhaps Grant Ogilvie would employ Ben and, finally, Mammy if he meant to live on the island occasionally.

She allowed the dinghy to drift towards the Bluff and round into Green Turtle Bay where the eternal run of the waves broke against the reef. At low tide the coral was fully exposed, forming a crescent of white foam between the Albatross Bank and the narrow entrance to the anchorage, and beyond it the bay looked like a sheet of glass. It was the perfect small lagoon, half hidden by its guardian reef, but it was hardly suitable for a commercial venture such as Grant Ogilvie undoubtedly proposed.

Makeda raised her eyes to the deserted house above the bay where she had first seen Grant's tall figure silhouetted in the doorway of Crichton's, and her heart turned over at the intensity of the memory. It was almost as if he were standing there now, tall and darkly arrogant, challenging her to turn him away.

She pulled the dinghy's head round to the sudden flurry of wind which came in across the Bluff, letting it fill the sail and bear her away.

The others were swimming in the cove when she finally dropped the sail and tied the dinghy to the jetty rail. Simon, his fair hair already bleaching in the sun, swam towards her.

'I thought you were going to work like a beaver all morning,' he called out when they were within hailing distance. 'There's not much sign of it, so far !'

'I—had to get away to think,' she told him as he waded through the bright green water, 'but I do mean to get down to the notes as quickly as possible. Have you had a nice swim?'

'Glorious !' He shook the surplus water from his hair. 'How far did you go?'

She shrugged.

'Not far. Out to the Dutchman's Cap and back to the Bluff, where I lost most of the wind.'

'Jacinthe thought she saw you going into Green Turtle Bay.'

'You sound as if you've been spying on me!' she laughed. 'Why shouldn't I go into Green Turtle, if I want to?'

'No reason, though according to Jacinthe it's badly haunted!'

'Oh, bother that!' Makeda exclaimed. 'She means Crichton's, of course. It's practically ruined now, although it was once the old plantation house for the island.' She wrapped the sail round the boom, coiling the sheets carefully on the slatted seats of the dinghy. 'Nobody believes in haunts any more, except Mammy.'

'When you didn't put in an appearance at breakfast Mammy thought you'd been spirited away overnight by Grant Ogilvie,' Simon offered lightly. 'She thinks he's not going to bring any good to the island.'

Makeda turned towards the house.

'He's been good enough to let us stay at Succoth in the meantime,' she pointed out. 'Perhaps I should remember that and get on with my work. Have you seen Heber?'

'He went down to the village early, to fish, I think.' Simon flung himself on to the warm sand. 'Don't go in just yet, Makeda,' he begged. 'Stay and swim for a while.'

'Later,' Makeda promised. 'It's almost time for elevenses.'

'I'll give Jacinthe a shout,' he offered, getting lazily to his feet. 'What a little porpoise she is! It took me all my time to keep up with her. She swims like a seal.'

'Make up your mind,' she teased. 'Seals and porpoises are completely different species!'

He tried to catch her as she ran up the beach.

'You've left your clothes behind!' she laughed, evading him easily enough. 'Don't forget to call Jacinthe!'

On her way across the garden she met Mammy.

'Miss Makeda, where yo' been?' the Carib woman demanded. 'Not one bite o' breakfast have passed yo' lips, I reckon, an' you away so early, an' all!'

'I'm ready to make up for it now,' Makeda assured her. 'I sailed out to the Dutchman's Cap and back by Green Turtle.'

'Don' you go near that Green Turtle Bay,' Mammy warned. 'Yo' be in bad trouble if yo' do. That Crichton's is fair haunted, an' no mistake. Ben, he see ol' Samuel Crichton standin' up there again jus' before yo' all went to Bridgetown. He see him as large as life in his red shirt wi' sleeves rolled up like he was gonna use his whip.'

'Mammy!' Makeda protested, 'that wasn't Samuel Crichton, or his ghost, since you believe there is one. It was Mr Ogilvie when he first came to the island. I saw him, too.'

She hesitated, watching some of the fear disappearing from the Carib woman's eyes, but Mammy was adept at the art of producing the last word.

'Well then, Miss Makeda,' she said, 'yo' jus' take warnin'. A man as like another man can't be all that different. Samuel Crichton was a bad tyrant an' yo' Mr Ogilvie wants to send us all away from Millo, an' where will we go?'

Makeda put her arm round her shoulders.

'Don't worry too much, Mammy,' she said. 'We'll find a way out. We'll take care of you and Ben and the children.'

Mammy hid her face in her apron.

'Yes, yo' will,' she said, as if to convince them both. 'I sure yo' will, Miss Makeda.'

Dolly was standing on the verandah when Makeda reached the house.

'What was all that about?' she wanted to know.

'Mammy was a bit upset,' Makeda confessed. 'Naturally enough, she doesn't want to leave Millo.' Suddenly she was looking her mother straight in the eye. 'When we have to leave, what will you do?'

Dolly didn't have to consider the question.

'I'll go with Heber. What else?' she said.

'Have you discussed it with him?'

'Not exactly, but Heber and I are very close. Wherever he goes, I intend to go with him. He is my son.'

'One day he'll want to marry,' Makeda pointed out. 'He'll want to be free.'

Dolly flushed.

'It's something we needn't worry about at the moment,' she declared.

'He'll be a fully qualified geologist in a year's time,'

Makeda persisted, 'which means that he'll look for work wherever he can find it—anywhere in the world, as a matter of fact. He may even become "a wanderer on the face of the earth", following his profession wherever it takes him. Would you really want to hang around under these circumstances?'

'I could make a home for him in Barbados or even in England, if that was what he wanted,' said Dolly. 'And you could come with us—you and Jacinthe. You'd get to know London and like it in a very short time.'

'I don't think so,' Makeda answered. 'I like it well enough, but not as a permanent home, and I can't imagine Jacinthe there, either.'

'Jacinthe is much too young to decide these things for herself,' Dolly said in an arbitrary tone. 'She has a career to think about, too. She must be trained for something, like you and Abi.'

'Yes, I suppose I could get a secretarial job,' Makeda reflected. 'I type well enough, and I can spell. That must be all there is to it.'

'You could always think about getting married,' Dolly suggested archly. 'If you're so keen on spending the rest of your life on Millo, what about Grant Ogilvie? He would make a good husband for you.'

'How could he?' Makeda cried passionately. 'We would never be able to see eye to eye if we lived on the same island for a hundred years!'

Dolly looked alarmed.

'Why do you dislike him so much?' she asked. 'He seems quite nice to me. In fact, he was perfectly willing to help in an emergency if I ever had to leave you here alone.'

'Mother, you haven't *asked* him?' Makeda gasped. 'You couldn't possibly do a thing like that, making us dependent on him.'

'But surely we are?' said Dolly. 'Without his agreement we couldn't stay here, even to finish your father's book.'

It was true; it was humiliatingly true, Makeda acknowledged, forgetting to ask about Mammy and Ben, which had been her main reason for opening the conversation in the first place.

For the next two days she applied herself to her work, leaving Heber and Jacinthe to entertain their guest. Heber seemed suddenly restless and Jacinthe's preoccupation with her own thoughts was more pronounced than ever. She went for long walks by herself up over the Bluff, and once Makeda saw her returning from Green Turtle Bay. If she had been to Crichton's she omitted to mention the fact, although she did make some reference to the mahogany trees.

'It isn't an avenue any more,' was what she actually said. 'It's all swallowed up by that dreadful scrub.'

'If we didn't hack it back at Succoth we'd be overpowered, too,' Heber remarked. 'If Grant comes back I think I'll ask him for a job.'

They all turned to gaze at him.

'I'll get swine fever or some disease if I go on doing nothing,' he explained with a grin. 'We're all layabouts around here except Makeda, and she has a Cause!'

'What sort of job had you in mind?' Makeda asked.

'If he's going to build over at Green Turtle I could lend a hand.'

'What a splendid idea!' Dolly approved. 'You mean just for your vacation, of course.'

He nodded.

'Supposing Grant doesn't come back?' Makeda asked.

'Oh, he'll come,' her brother declared. 'He told me I could start nailing Succoth together, if I had a mind to. Simon, you could help me with the porch this afternoon,' he suggested.

Simon shifted his position on the cane lounger to look at Makeda.

'What about your father's notes?' he asked. 'I've been jotting down a few facts from memory which might prove useful once we'd compared them,' he added.

Makeda's eyes brightened.

'It would be more useful than helping Heber with the porch,' she said.

Jacinthe went off over the Bluff again. It was as if she were waiting for someone.

Grant? The thought struck Makeda like a blow between the eyes, but surely Grant had no time for anyone but his 'Beautiful Lady'? Poor Jacinthe!

'If you mean to help,' she told Simon sharply, 'I'm starting right away.'

He followed her into the house and along the back corridor to the room overlooking the scrub where her father's desk stood by the window. It was covered by his notes and the reference books she had been using.

'Do we clear the decks first, or do you prefer to work in a perpetual muddle?' he asked.

'I've been trying to get things into reasonable order for two days,' she confessed, 'but it will take me a while longer. My father never numbered his pages, for one thing, and this final batch of notes is hard to follow. There are missing sections which will probably turn up towards the end, all out of sequence, of course.'

He leaned across the table, lifting the heavy sheaf of papers which Grant Ogilvie had returned to her when she had left it in the lawyer's office, and a small flicker of resentment stirred in Makeda's heart. It was foolish, she thought, to feel so sensitive, especially with someone like Simon who was so eager to help.

They spent the next two hours going over the first section of the MS. It was the part she had worked on with her father and a thousand memories crowded into her mind, leaving her quieter than usual. It was also very hot in the room, although the jalousies had been thrown wide to catch what air there was, and at three o'clock she decided that they had done enough. Her father's desk was cleared of a collection of unnecessary papers and the relevant notes and files were now in order, ranged in neat rows on a table along one wall.

Simon mopped his brow.

'So much for that,' he said. 'How about a swim now?'

'Ask Jacinthe,' Makeda advised. 'I think I'll go for a walk.'

'A walk in this weather? You must be very keen,' he protested.

'It does you good to stretch your legs.'

'You could stretch them swimming. I haven't been round

to the Atlantic side of the island yet.'

'Jacinthe will take you.'

'I dare say.' He gave her an odd look. 'You really mean you don't want to come?'

She nodded.

The truth was that she very much wanted to be alone. As she read through the first part of the MS again, her father had come very near and she was half-way over the Bluff before she realised where her steps were taking her. Simon had gone off in search of Jacinthe and she had turned the opposite way almost automatically.

It was a stiff climb in such heat, but soon she was on the topmost crag looking down into Green Turtle Bay where *Seafarer* lay reflected in the placid water of the lagoon.

The fact that the ketch was there was no great surprise to her. She had felt it in her bones ever since she had left Succoth, but she had no intention of going on to confront Grant on his own doorstep, so to speak. During their first encounter they had marked out their separate territories, it seemed; Green Turtle and Frenchman's with the craggy barrier of the Bluff in between, and she was determined to keep it that way until she finally left Millo for good.

There was no sign of life on the ketch and she allowed herself a moment's respite before she turned to retrace her steps to the other side of the Bluff. Green Turtle looked very peaceful lying down there in the sun, with the grove of coconut palms casting slanting shadows across the beach and the waves breaking in a fine white line along the reef. Above her, half hidden by the encroaching scrub, Grant Ogilvie was sitting on a convenient boulder, reading a letter.

Makeda saw him when she turned to go back to Succoth and her swiftly-indrawn breath appeared to carry across the still air to him, disturbing his concentration.

'That was a strategic move,' he said, rising to join her. 'Do you always creep up on your adversaries from behind, Sheba?'

'I wish you wouldn't call me that!' she protested. 'I'm very proud of my name, but it is Makeda.'

'I stand corrected.' He smiled at her. 'Did you come about

anything specific?' He looked down at *Seafarer*.

'No.' Her blunt denial seemed to stand in the air between them. 'I'm sorry if I'm intruding.'

He handed over the letter he had been reading.

'You may as well look at it,' he said. 'I had no idea the lease of Millo had only three more years to run.'

Makeda thrust the paper back at him.

'It doesn't concern me,' she pointed out unsteadily. 'In three years' time I'll be very far away.'

He left her remark unanswered.

'It was a lot of money to pay for such a short lease,' he observed. 'Which makes me more convinced than ever that my uncle just wanted to be generous to an old friend.'

A dull red colour flooded into Makeda's cheeks.

'Which is something you wouldn't be able to understand!' she retorted to cover her humiliation.

'On the contrary,' he said, all the mockery gone out of his voice, 'if it hadn't been for George Hunt I would probably be earning a precarious living in a city somewhere. Possibly England.'

'I couldn't imagine it,' she declared. 'This sort of life suits you.'

'For once we're agreed.' He walked through the shrub by her side. 'I intend to apply for a renewal of the lease, of course,' he told her, 'and meanwhile, I'll go ahead with the plans I already have for Millo.'

She wanted more than anything to ask about these plans, but emotion kept her tongue in check this time.

'I mean to rebuild Crichton's,' Grant said, looking across the bay to where the giant mahogany trees caught the light of the departing sun. 'I mean to live there.'

'At Crichton's?' For a moment it seemed wholly incredible to Makeda. 'Oh, I see!' she said in the next instant, 'you would feel you had something to show for your wealth if you owned an old plantation house.'

Grant laughed outright.

'You do me an injustice, Sheba,' he returned lightly. 'A show of "wealth" never occurred to me, and if it did I daresay I could have found some other place to proclaim it, somewhere less secluded than Millo, don't you think?'

'You said you mean to live here.' Her curiosity got the better of her. 'It will be years and years before you're able to restore it to the Crichton's it was.'

'Not necessarily,' he said. 'I've laid most of that on, as a matter of fact. I've a trader coming over from Grenada on Thursday with the beams for the roof and other essentials to make a start. The rest I can bring in on *Seafarer* as I go along.'

'A trader would never get into Green Turtle,' she pointed out. 'The gap in the reef is too narrow and not nearly deep enough.'

'That's what I was about to ask. Would you give me the use of Frenchman's Cove?'

'I couldn't refuse you. The whole island is yours,' she answered reluctantly.

'Frenchman's would mean right on your doorstep,' he pointed out, 'but it needn't be a desperate inconvenience.'

'If you landed your heavy cargo at Frenchman's you'd never get it across the Bluff.'

He smiled thinly.

'Don't put too many obstacles in my way, Sheba,' he said. 'There used to be a track between Succoth and Crichton's, I understand. It went over the low ground and down into Green Turtle Bay.'

'And it's been buried in scrub ever since we came here,' she told him.

'The scrub could be cleared.'

'It would be a monumental task.'

'But not insurmountable.' He put the letter from his uncle's solicitor back into his pocket. 'Anyway, I mean to have a go.'

'Alone?'

'That would be impossible. No, I have at least two willing assistants, an architect friend from Barbados and your brother. Heber has asked me for a job during his vacation and I can hire labour from the village to clear the scrub. Quite a few of the fishermen have offered to come along when I need them.'

'I had no idea you were so far advanced with your plans. Heber mentioned that he would ask you for a job, but I didn't think he'd got round to it,' she confessed.

'We had a long talk about Crichton's on our way back from Barbados,' Grant explained. 'I threw out a few hints after Heber had spoken about finding something to do in the long vacation. Don't think this is some sort of treachery on Heber's part,' he added. 'It will keep your mother happy if he stays on the island and he'll be working for Millo. He has the same feeling about restoring Crichton's as I have. It will be something of the past lifted into the present and made useful again.'

'When you've finished restoring the house what will you do?' she asked. 'Will you feel that you've satisfied another ambition and leave Millo to its own devices?'

'Restoring a place like Crichton's doesn't just mean putting a roof on the house and making it habitable,' he answered. 'The whole estate must be brought gradually back into cultivation. Sugar is too precarious a crop nowadays to work on one's own, but I have a mind to grow pineapple and spices. The north of the island is very fertile and what workforce I would need could be brought over from Grenada or St Vincent to enlarge the village. Huts are easy enough to build, and Morgan's Reach would be an ideal spot for a settlement.'

Makeda's pulses had quickened as she listened. It was all and more than she could have hoped for the island.

'I envy you,' she told him truthfully, her voice not quite steady. 'It's the sort of thing I would have liked to do for Millo.'

He didn't answer that.

'How is the book coming on?' he asked instead.

'Fairly well. Simon is helping me now.'

He frowned.

'How long is he here for?'

'Could be till my father's book is finished.'

The frown deepened.

'Does he really know enough about the dig to co-operate so

wholeheartedly?' he asked bluntly. 'I understand he was only there during the second half of the exploration.'

Makeda stiffened.

'I don't think that makes any difference,' she said. 'How *long* he was there. He seems to know his job, and he's jotted down all sorts of impressions of his own which could be helpful.'

'Fair enough,' he agreed almost indifferently. 'So long as you trust him. Until about a week ago he was no more than a vague background figure as far as you were concerned.'

'You *can* get to know people in a week!' Makeda protested.

'You can form an impression,' he corrected her. 'Getting to know people is something quite different, Sheba.'

'You think I'm ready to fall into any trap!' she exclaimed angrily. 'I'm not a child. I'm eighteen!'

'As much as that?' His eyebrows were raised incredulously as he looked down into her eyes with the old mockery in his own. 'I could have thought you were younger, but never mind! You'll grow up one day and then I may tell you what I really think.'

'I won't be on Millo to hear you,' she protested stormily.

'I think you will,' he said. 'Growing up can happen in a day.'

He escorted her through the scrub to the place where the old road between Crichton's and Succoth could just be seen on the low side of the Bluff. The land sloped away here, rising again towards Pelican Head in the east where the Atlantic swell came rushing in. Farther north, at Morgan's Reach, they could see the roofs of the fishing village which Grant hoped to enlarge, and all at once it seemed to come to life for Makeda. There was the road connecting Crichton Place with Succoth, and there was the trodden path to a thriving settlement where the Carib fishermen would live peaceably with the families Grant brought in to work on the estate. All the rich, sloping ground in between would be cultivated, with the stiff spears of the pineapples in regimental rows marching across the valley to the headland in the west. Succoth and the land to the south of it would yield the spices, while beyond Crichton's mahogany trees would replace the scrub right down to the water's edge. She could visualise it quite clearly, although it was something she would never see.

'The two estates could be run very well with a manager at Succoth,' said Grant.

'When you marry,' she suggested, hardly able to trust her voice because he had allowed her this glimpse of Millo as it could become. 'You said you meant to live at Crichton's eventually.'

'That's my intention,' he agreed without answering the first part of her question. 'It wasn't such a big house originally, but large enough to accommodate a family. I want it to look exactly as it did when the first Crichton had finished who earned himself a reputation as a tyrant.'

They had reached the edge of the scrub where the path went down to Succoth and he turned to retrace his steps across the Bluff.

'What happens when the trader comes in?' Makeda asked.

'I'll come across to help unload her. I'll be at Green Turtle aboard *Seafarer* most of the time till Crichton's is ready.'

It meant that he would be a permanent resident on the island now, the man in possession who could watch their every movement wherever they went from now on. She had been about to invite him to Succoth for a refreshing drink which anyone would have done in the circumstances, but she allowed him to go without a word.

'What did Grant want?' Heber asked, coming down the step-ladder which he had propped up against the rickety porch.

'He would like you to start work at Crichton's,' said Makeda. 'Apparently you discussed it on *Seafarer* on your way across from Bridgetown.'

Heber looked delighted.

'Mind you, I'll finish off here before I go,' he promised.

'Are you going to paint the porch?' she asked.

'Simon promised to do that.'

'He's making himself indispensable around here!'

'Isn't that what you want?' Heber queried. 'I only need half an eye to see how infatuated he is.'

'Now you're being ridiculous,' Makeda said, turning away.

Was that what they all thought? That she and Simon were attracted to one another? Of course, he was attentive and thoroughly charming, with a way of precipitating her into a situation before she had fully considered its implications, but she had never dreamed that it was so obvious to her family, at least. Heber hadn't said whether he approved or disapproved. It was only Grant Ogilvie who had warned her about forming impressions too hastily.

Well, she had to work with Simon now that they had begun, and what he thought about her didn't really matter. What was important was their race to finish her father's book before Grant decided to compile his uncle's notes for another one.

For the next two days they worked hard, with only the odd swim out across the Cove to punctuate their efforts. Makeda had lost her former inhibitions about allowing her father's papers to be scrutinised by a comparative stranger primarily because Simon had produced much useful material of his own. He insisted, however, that she should handle the final batch of notes herself, aware, no doubt, of her sensitive approach to the matter.

'I don't really mind now,' she told him on the day the trader made its first appearance in Frenchman's Cove. 'We've been working well together, Simon. You're not a stranger any more.'

He put down his pen to consider the matter.

'I believe your mother feels the same way,' he said carefully. 'I don't really think she wants to see the back of me.'

'What will you do when all this is finished?' she asked.

He hesitated for only a moment.

'I'd like to write,' he confessed. 'To go on writing, I should say. This has been a wonderful experience for me, Makeda, and certainly there's a lot more to be said about your father's subject. Oh, I know dozens of people have put their theories into print, but there's always room for more.' He bent over the table where she was typing the first draft of the MS. 'We could even go into partnership,' he suggested. 'Your father used to call me "the Fledgling", you know, and I do have a lot to learn, but we've both got the bug, Makeda. We could join an expedition together.'

'Hi, wait a bit,' Makeda protested. 'I don't know half enough for that sort of thing. I'm interested because it was my father's job, but that's all. Honestly, it is. There was nothing much for me to do but tidy up his notes while he "dug his way to Ophir", as mother put it, but apart from that I'm completely ignorant and untrained.'

'Experience is the best training,' he said. 'Besides, you would have your father's name to back you up. It would be half way to success as far as you were concerned.'

'I couldn't trade on a thing like that.' Makeda rose to put her work away. 'I've always wanted to stand on my own two feet.'

They walked through to the verandah to look out at the trader.

'Ogilvie is taking possession in a big way,' Simon remarked. 'What's he going to do with all that wood?'

'Re-roof Crichton's. The original beams were made of oak.'

Two days earlier the men from the village had started their onslaught on the scrub, slashing the giant bushes with machetes and burning it as they went along. The heavy smell of wood smoke had enveloped the island, drifting far out to sea on the prevailing wind until it must have looked as if Millo was on fire.

'We almost went back for the fire brigade!' the jovial skipper of the *Fair Trader* announced when they went down to speak to him. 'You've certainly got a new broom on the island these days, Miss Garland.'

'How are you going to get all this stuff ashore?' Makeda asked. 'You can't come in to the jetty.'

'We've got a pontoon. Mr Ogilvie thought it out. At high tide we can come in a bit farther and if we lie up close we can put an extension on to the jetty.'

'I told you Ogilvie thinks of everything,' Simon said at Makeda's elbow.

'It's quite sensible if it works,' she declared. 'I suppose Heber will want everyone to help. Where's Jacinthe, by the way?'

Jacinthe had been going off on her own frequently these past few days, often returning from the direction of Crichton's, much to Makeda's dismay. I hope she's not going to fall in love with him, she thought, remembering how ruthless Grant was. It would be disastrous!

'Here comes our Master of Works!' said Simon, recognising Heber as he came down from the cleared part of the road. 'He may know about Jacinthe. Certainly I don't.'

'Jacinthe?' Heber asked. 'I guess she's having a bout of the sulks. Haven't you noticed recently how touchy she is? I can't raise a laugh with her, whatever I do.'

When Jacinthe did come into view Grant was with her. He had changed out of his working clothes into a more presentable pair of trousers and had put on a shirt, something he had cast aside while working on the road. He shook hands with the trader's skipper, measuring him with his usual directness.

'What do you think, Captain?' he asked diplomatically. 'Are we going to be able to work with the pontoon?'

'I've been giving it a bit of thought.' The skipper scratched his head. 'We could try it out in the morning and see how it goes.'

Grant nodded.

'I think it ought to work,' he said.

'I'd like to have taken your passenger into Green Turtle,' the skipper remarked, 'but it was a mite risky. Will you be coming aboard, Mr Ogilvie?'

'Passenger?' Grant looked puzzled as he turned towards the jetty, but Makeda had already seen the girl aboard the *Fair Trader*. She was standing at the head of the companion-way leading from the cabins, a tall girl with an elegance about her that was unmistakable. Dressed for the voyage from Grenada in pale blue slacks and a tomato-red suede waistcoat over her blue silk shirt, she wore vivid tomato-coloured deck shoes, while her fair hair was bound by a blue cotton kerchief tied in a knot at the back. No one, Makeda thought, could fail to recognise Grant's 'Beautiful Lady'.

He went straight down the beach towards her, jumping into the dinghy which the skipper had used to come ashore and rowing vigorously until he reached the trader's side. The girl in the suede waistcoat bent down to talk to him as Makeda turned in the direction of Succoth.

'Aren't you going to stay to see the wood come off?' Heber asked. 'We may need an extra hand.'

'I've got other things to do.' Makeda was half-way up the beach. 'Mammy may need some help in the kitchen.'

'I've never known it!' Heber returned, giving her an odd look. 'Please yourself, though, but we certainly could do with extra help down here when we start to unload.'

Simon said: 'What's the hurry, Makeda? It's only four o'clock.'

She hesitated, half way up the beach. It did look as if she was running away, and Jacinthe had already disappeared. She had merged into the shadows of the coconut grove as if she had never been on the beach at all.

Grant was rowing the dinghy back from the trader with his unexpected visitor sitting in the stern, his long, powerful strokes sending the little craft across the still green water as if it had been a skiff. Eager hands hauled it up the beach so that the Beautiful Lady needn't get her feet wet.

As soon as he had shipped his oars Grant went into the water, offering her his hand.

She was the most fascinating person Makeda had ever seen. The dimly-lit restaurant in Bridgetown had done her less than justice and now, with the last of the sun on it, her hair was a deep, rich chestnut and not black, as it had seemed in the artificial light. Her features were flawless and she had a perfect skin just faintly powdered with freckles where the sun had caught it, but what was even more disconcerting was the fact that she seemed to be completely at ease in her present surroundings.

'I couldn't wait to see it, Grant!' she exclaimed as he lifted her clear of the dinghy to deposit her on the beach. 'I had to come right away out of sheer curiosity. I promise you I won't interfere,' she laughed. 'Not at this stage, but you can picture me thinking of Crichton's all this time and not being able to see it.'

'I can well imagine your inquisitiveness,' Grant agreed, picking up the large canvas folder she had brought with her. 'What have you in here?'

'Lots and lots of clever ideas. I haven't been idle since last we met!' she declared.

'Apparently.' Grant turned to the others. 'I want you to meet Heber Garland,' he said. 'He's going to help us with Crichton's. Heber, this is Helen Rossiter. Helen—Simon Wetherby and Makeda.'

Makeda held out her hand.

'I hope you'll like it here,' she said automatically. 'It's really very quiet.'

'Isn't that what everyone is looking for nowadays?' Helen turned to smile at her. 'How glorious Millo is! I can't quite believe it. Grant tells me you've lived here for most of your life, but he hasn't told me half enough about the island itself. I shall want to explore every inch of it so that I can't go wrong when I'm working on the house.'

A tight hand seemed to clamp down on Makeda's heart. It was true. It was painfully true! This was the girl Grant was going to marry. When he had said 'I mean to rebuild Crichton's. I mean to live here', he had been thinking of Helen Rossiter living with him up there at the restored plantation house. He had been thinking in terms of a more settled way of life for himself and the girl who would be his wife.

She could not look at Grant standing by Helen's side because of the sudden pain in her heart, the ache which said, 'I love you! I love you!'

But Grant had never loved her. He had treated her as a child because she had behaved like a child, but now that was all over. When Helen Rossiter had walked up the beach by Grant's side she had recognised the extent of her own passion, the irresistible attraction which had taken her, again and again, to Green Turtle Bay. I'm in love with him, she thought, and I must stay here and watch while he builds Crichton's for someone else.

A surge of tempestuous emotion rose in her heart, filling her eyes with the tears she could no longer hold at bay nor banish clean away, and the thought of Jacinthe and Grant seemed ridiculous now that Helen had come on the scene. Jacinthe and she were both immature adolescents compared with this beautiful, sophisticated woman of the world who had followed Grant into the wilderness.

There was nothing about Helen Rossiter that she could fairly dislike. It was only her own foolish heart that was so full of envy as she watched Helen making friends with the others. Heber had gone down before the newcomer's charm like a ton of bricks, as he himself would have said, and even Simon was impressed.

'There's so much to do,' Helen declared, looking about her with knowledgeable eyes. 'I see you've already started on the road, Grant. Does that mean that we can get the roof beams over right away?'

'Almost,' Grant told her. 'I've been agreeably surprised at the way everyone has worked, especially the fishermen. They seemed a lazy crew till I explained my plans to them, but they very soon became enthusiastic. They'll have the wood across the Bluff in next to no time once the road is complete.'

'It's passable now,' said Heber, standing next to Helen. 'You can walk all the way to Crichton's without having to hack out your trail with a machete. Would you like to go over there?' he asked eagerly. 'I could take you right away and we could be back before sundown.'

Helen looked in Grant's direction with a whimsical smile.

'You've got all the enthusiasm you need to back you up without me!' she laughed. 'Do I go with Herber or do I wait till you've unloaded your cargo from the *Fair Trader*?'

Grant hesitated, considering the alternative.

'I'd like to take you,' he said. 'I'd like to be with you when you first see Crichton's.'

Suddenly Makeda felt as if her heart would break. Of course, he wanted to be there with Helen when she first saw their future home! Heber had been curiously insensitive when he had offered to accompany Helen on her journey over the Bluff, but perhaps he just didn't understand.

'You must come and meet my mother,' he said as they moved up the beach. 'She's sure to have seen us from the verandah at Succoth and she'll be consumed by curiosity to know who you are!'

'I'd like to meet her,' Helen said before they moved too far ahead for Makeda to overhear.

'Do I offer to lend a hand in the morning?' Simon asked, looking back to where Grant was studying the pontoon with Captain Bayley. 'All hands to the plough, or something!'

'All hands to the oars would be more appropriate!' Makeda endeavoured to sound suitably amused. 'I suppose we ought to offer since everyone else is leaning over backwards to be helpful.'

'Especially Heber, do you mean?'

Makeda swallowed hard.

'Heber and—the others,' she said harshly. 'Crichton's seems to be all that really matters just now.'

'Hold on, Makeda!' he protested. 'It's not like you to be so biased. I only thought we might put in a couple of hours for appearances' sake to show no ill-feeling, but if you don't really see things that way we needn't offer. We're more than half-way through with the MS,' he added tentatively, 'so one morning would be neither here nor there.'

Half-way through, Makeda thought; not so very far from the end of her task and the end of her life on Millo. In two or three weeks' time she would be gone, leaving her beloved island to flourish under a stranger's hand aided by a girl she could not really hate.

The pain of the thought went all the way back to Succoth with her where Dolly was sitting alone on the verandah, waiting for news of the stranger. Apparently, Helen had agreed to go to Crichton's with Heber.

'Wherever is she going to stay?' Dolly asked. 'Grant can't

put her up at Crichton's before he has a roof on the place, and she can't live on board his boat.'

'People do these things nowadays,' Makeda answered abruptly. 'They're probably engaged.'

'I don't think that should make any difference,' Dolly returned. 'I'll have a word with Grant about it.'

'I wouldn't,' Makeda warned. 'He'll tell you in the nicest possible way to mind your own business.'

'Really, Makeda!' her mother protested. 'You don't know him at all.'

'I think I do,' said Makeda, her voice all blurred with pain. 'He's completely sure of himself and what he wants to do, and —and if he loved someone he wouldn't care a jot what anyone thought about his actions.'

'Makeda!'

'I'm sorry, but you know it's true,' Makeda said. 'He would be his own judge and that would be an end to it.'

'You may be right,' Dolly agreed, 'although there's no need for you to be so vehement about it. I had a notion that you two might get to know each other a little better,' she added, 'and one day you could have settled here, but if Grant is already engaged that puts a new complexion on everything.'

'Mother, please don't go on,' begged Makeda, all the colour going out of her face. ' "One day" is only a dream, something futile and silly now that we've discovered the truth. Grant Ogilvie could never have loved me, not in a thousand years. I put paid to that from the beginning, even if he hadn't been in love with someone else.'

'My dear child!' Dolly felt hopelessly inadequate to deal with a situation which she did not wholly understand. 'You don't mean——'

Makeda had gone before she could complete her sentence and Dolly was left on the verandah to reflect that nothing was so odd as the ways of people in love.

CHAPTER SIX

FOR three days the *Fair Trader* remained in Frenchman's Cove while the pontoon was moored into position and her cargo of wood was slowly unloaded on to the beach, from where it was carted laboriously over the new and sometimes inadequate road to Crichton Place on the far side of the Bluff.

Helen, when she finally came to Succoth, refused Dolly's offer of accommodation in the nicest possible way, explaining that she would be returning to Grenada with the trader and was going back to Barbados by air. There was no point, therefore, in removing all her belongings from the comfortable cabin she occupied in the *Fair Trader* to sleep ashore for so short a time.

'When I come again,' she said, 'I'll be only too grateful for your hospitality, Mrs Garland, if it's still available to me.'

It was the type of courtesy Dolly appreciated, although at first she had thought that Heber was paying too much attention to the fascinating newcomer. If Helen was going to marry Grant Ogilvie there could be little fear of her setting her very attractive cap at an impoverished student who had no great prospects ahead of him.

Makeda began to work feverishly at her father's book, almost as if she had to end her sojourn on Millo as quickly as possible. The prolonged pain of living so close to Grant and his Beautiful Lady grew sharper every day and work seemed the only solution. She plunged into it with a ruthlessness which everyone acknowledged as typical, yet each word she wrote, each paragraph duly completed, was bringing her nearer to the moment of departure.

Simon, at this period of their mutual effort, seemed less inclined to forge ahead without delay, allowing his interest to stray to Crichton's and all that was happening there. It was an exciting time for the islanders, too, as they sang their way along the newly-restored road between Succoth and Green Turtle Bay, carrying their heavy loads on their powerful shoulders with amazing ease. They worked with a will for Grant, not only because he paid them well but because they respected and admired him. Any man who would take off his shirt and toil, stripped to the waist, side by side with his labourers, commanded their wholehearted allegiance, and before two days had passed most of the heavy timber was on the far side of the Bluff where Grant wanted it.

Working at Succoth, Makeda was ignorant of the progress he was making, although Heber submitted a detailed report to her mother each evening before their meal.

'What does Miss Rossiter do over there all day long?' Dolly asked when most of the wood had been removed from the beach.

'*Mrs* Rossiter,' Heber corrected. 'Her husband must be dead, since she's been working for herself for some time now. She's a qualified architect, among other things.'

Makeda looked up to meet her mother's surprised gaze.

'A widow!' said Dolly.

'Does that make a difference?' Heber looked amused as he poured himself a drink.

'I don't suppose so, although I would have thought——'

'That Grant would have selected a male architect?' Heber laughed. 'It wouldn't make a blessed bit of difference to him so long as they were right for Crichton's. Helen knows what he wants and she's extremely competent. Grant gave her the job of restoring Crichton Place to its former glory because he knew she would do it well. She has a lot of knowledge about the period we're dealing with, so her experience is invaluable to him.'

'But is he in love with her?' Dolly persisted. 'On the face of it, I think he must be.'

'Your reasoning was always a bit cock-eyed, Mother,' her son declared. 'Perhaps he is and perhaps he isn't. One couldn't really tell with Grant. It's the sort of thing he would keep to himself until it was relevant to release it for public approval.'

'She would make a wonderful mistress for Crichton's,' Dolly reflected. 'Can't you picture her coming down the grand staircase in a flowing gown with her hair up and that calm look in her eyes which seems to be her personal hallmark?'

Makeda rose hastily to her feet.

'What's the matter?' Dolly demanded. 'You do jump about a lot these days, Makeda! Where are you going?'

'I've just thought of something I have to do.' Makeda's voice was harsh with constriction. 'It won't take more than half an hour.'

To escape for a moment, to run away from all this talk about Grant and his Beautiful Lady, was suddenly essential to her if she was not going to give herself away completely to sharp-eyed Heber or even her mother, whose curiosity had already penetrated part of her defences.

She chose the narrow path over the Bluff, which was used less frequently now that the road through the scrub was open, because up here, with the soft trade wind in her face and the sun on her hair, she might find some sort of solace for her wounded spirit.

How had she come to love him? There was no point at which she could say here or there. It had been a slow and gradual process over those difficult weeks when she had refused to come to terms with the fact of his inheritance and the knowledge that her beloved island was now his by right. The transfer of Millo had been hard enough to bear, but the transfer of her love from the island to the man who now owned it was something she had yet to contend with in the fuller sense. I can't love him, she thought desperately, again and again. I mustn't! It would be too cruel, too terrible a thing to live with all my life. She had thought of Jacinthe in love with Grant, feeling sorry for her, although Jacinthe was no more than a schoolgirl, but suddenly she understood all that her cousin must have suffered if Grant had rejected her. First love was a terrible thing, and no wonder people called it a traumatic experience which could never truly be forgotten. It was deep and sensitive and so easily torn apart; it was complete and utter trust or it was pain beyond enduring. It was the culmination of a thousand dreams which had taken shape gradually in a young girl's heart. Only to be shattered? Always shattered by reality?

She reached the highest point of the Bluff where she could look down into Green Turtle Bay, finding it as it had always been, lonely and isolated except for *Seafarer* rocking at anchor in the rapidly fading light.

'What do you think of our efforts up to now?' Grant asked from the shadows of a clump of sage. 'It was something you thought we couldn't do.'

She turned swiftly at the sound of his voice.

'You appear from nowhere,' she accused him, trying to hide her shock at his unexpected presence. 'You've certainly made contact between the two bays possible and you appear to have all your building material where you want it. When do you start on the roof?'

'Immediately.' He came to stand on the rock beside her. 'While there's plenty of labour available I intend to forge ahead. Once the roof is on we can take our time.'

'Helen Rossiter will help you, I suppose.'

'That was the main idea. She's a clever architect and a very old friend.'

'Apart from being the most beautiful person I've ever seen,' Makeda added, torturing herself because the truth had always been essential to her. 'She's not like anyone else I know.'

'To which I would say "amen". She thinks you may not like her, Sheba. Why is that?' he demanded, looking down at her with a penetrating scowl.

'I haven't given her any reason to believe I'm—jealous of her, or anything like that,' Makeda defended herself.

'But are you jealous?'

She turned her back on him.

'Not in the way you mean,' she said. 'I know I could never look like her if I tried for a thousand years, and she has all the attributes that go with complete confidence.'

'You're not saying you're less than sure of yourself?' he smiled.

She turned back to look at him, her head held unconsciously high.

'I don't want to wrangle any more,' she announced, steadying her voice with an effort. 'All I want to do is to get on with my work so that I can send my father's MS off to the publishers as quickly as possible. Then—then it won't matter so much if I have to go. I've made up my mind to it now, even though you haven't come to spoil Millo by building an outsize hotel on every beach.'

'That was your original impression, I remember,' he mused, 'but now you seem to be reconciled to the fact that you were wrong, although you haven't apologised.'

'If you want to hear me say "I'm sorry" then I will.' She met his inquisitive gaze with a supreme effort. 'I'm sorry I misjudged you when you first came here, but you didn't exactly make things easy for me. You didn't tell me the truth in the beginning.'

'Because you were too busy jumping to conclusions.' He came a little nearer. 'Sheba, you're still a child. You still protest too much, but I think you know now that I'll never spoil Millo. It will always be just as you've known it, and if you want more time at Succoth you can have that, too.'

'No, I couldn't!' she cried. 'When I've finished the book I'll go, as I promised.'

He drew in a deep breath.

'I wanted to speak to you about the book,' he said unexpectedly, 'and perhaps this is as good a time to do it as any. I still think we should pool our resources. It might be easier for us to co-operate rather than remain enemies when there's so much at stake. I offered you the use of my uncle's notes a long time ago and you refused, but I think you owe it to your father's memory to take a look at them, at least. There are passages in them which I frankly don't understand, but with your particular knowledge you might be able to read enough into them to make them worthwhile. That way they would pay dividends.'

She stiffened perceptibly.

'Why should I help you if you consider this as a successful business venture?' she demanded coldly. 'It would be something else to add to your empire, I suppose, something to achieve apart from building successful concrete palaces all over the Islands!'

He caught her by the arm and she felt the hard grip of his fingers as they fastened over her bare flesh. Anger was written all over his dark countenance and his eyes were as cold as steel.

'On the contrary,' he said, 'my affection for my uncle is two-fold—admiration for the work he did without acclaim and gratitude for his affection, which you may not believe possible. Jacinthe feels much the same about your parents, by the way,' he added, 'although you may not have stopped to consider the fact. We want to *do* things for a family which has shown us kindness, that's all.'

He did not wait for her to answer, striding off in the direction of Succoth in the assumption that she would follow close behind. It was almost dark now, with most of the colour gone out of the sky. The afterglow of sunset had flared and disappeared, leaving nothing but the swift darkness of the tropic night to embrace the headland and the paler sands below. There was no moon to guide them and very few stars.

Presently Grant came back to look for her.

'Go carefully,' he cautioned. 'We disturbed some of the rock when we re-made the road.'

At Succoth he said, almost dismissively:

'You can find your own way from here, I dare say. I'm going on board the trader for a meal. Goodnight, Makeda. Once again, if you change your mind about my uncle's notes, let me know.'

He had conquered his anger, but he could not forget it. Makeda stood where he left her on the path to Succoth, her eyes dimmed by sudden tears. Had she made an enemy of

Grant for no true reason at all? The tension between them when they met was something she could not understand, but deep down she knew it to be a thing of her own making. Right from the beginning he had offered her the use of his uncle's notes with no strings attached, but a demon of perversity in her or some sort of foolish pride had urged her to reject his offer out of hand.

Simon was the only one who had seen her come in. He was standing in the dark shadows of the verandah, smoking a cheroot, when she finally ran up the shallow steps and he moved forward to block her way into the house.

'I didn't see you,' she said, endeavouring to keep her voice steady. 'Where are the others?'

'Heber and your mother have gone aboard the trader by special invitation from Captain Bayley. He's giving a small dinner-party to mark his departure and the successful completion of his contract.'

'I—saw Grant going over,' Makeda admitted. 'Where's Jacinthe?'

'In her room. She's a bit choked at not being asked to the dinner-party.'

'Neither were we,' Makeda pointed out. 'The cabin accommodation on the trader is limited.'

Simon said: 'It doesn't worry me,' in a matter-of-fact tone. 'I'd settle for Mammy's cooking any day—or yours.'

He put his arm about her shoulders, but Makeda was too raw from her encounter with Grant to encourage Simon's attentions.

'If Jacinthe has something else to do we could start on the final batch of notes?' she asked. 'We could have a couple of hours after dinner to get them sorted out for the morning.'

She preferred to work during the morning hours when a fresh approach could be brought to her task, but sorting though the papers her father had left was an automatic job which could be done at any time.

Simon pulled thoughtfully on his cheroot, his eyes on its glowing tip as he considered her suggestion.

'Why not?' he said at last, casting it over the verandah

rail where it made a small parabola of light before it fell into the encroaching scrub. 'We're fast approaching the moment of truth.'

'Do you think they really found what they were looking for?' Makeda asked. 'Some sort of mine? Even if it was already worked out it would be a valuable source of information and a terrific climax to the book.'

'I think they found something,' Simon agreed slowly. 'You've looked through the notes, of course?'

Makeda shook her head.

'Not properly. They were in a bit of a muddle and I like to take one step at a time. After all, that was how my father and Professor Hunt tackled the dig—one careful step at a time without really knowing what the next day's work would reveal. I thought if I compiled the MS in the same way it would read better in the end. There would always be a sense of impending discovery, of day-to-day endeavour, which was in fact the case.'

'If the notes had been mine I wouldn't have been able to resist at least a peek!' Simon laughed. 'You're a remarkable character, Makeda, and I'd take my hat off to you if I were wearing one! When it's all over,' he added abruptly, 'will you go to London or New York to wait for publication day?'

She had asked herself the same question many times without being able to reach a decision.

'I can't think of anything in New York that would interest me apart from the book,' she confessed, 'and London seems very far away.' Her heart would be wrenched in two when she was forced to make her final decision. 'Perhaps I want to take it step by step, not looking forward too far, just going on from day to day as my father did.'

He looked at her closely.

'Your mother doesn't want to stay on Millo a moment longer than it takes us to complete the MS,' he reminded her. 'She'll stay as long as Heber wants to be on the island, but if he changes his mind about working at Crichton's she'll bale out with him.'

'I know.' Makeda went ahead of him into the house. 'The

odd thing is that I believe Heber will stay the course. He's become very interested in Crichton's these past few days and he's worked terrifically hard. Even Mother couldn't convince him that he ought to go if he wanted to be here.'

'I suppose not. I wonder if the Ogilvie edict applies to your mother,' Simon reflected.

'That she must leave as soon as the book is complete? Yes, I think it does. After all, being here was only a provision in the original sale which Grant agreed to honour after his uncle died.'

'It's hardly costing him anything,' Simon observed dryly. 'He's putting a new roof on Crichton's for his own benefit, but he'll have to start repairing Succoth in a big way if it's to be habitable for the next few years.'

'I know,' Makeda acknowledged. 'It's been falling down about our ears for a long time, but so long as it was a roof my father didn't worry too much. You know what he was like. He could shut his mind to everything but his work and worry about things as they happened.'

'That was part of his charm,' Simon agreed, pausing in the dining-room doorway. 'Do you want me to light the lamps in here?'

'Mammy has put candles on the table,' said Makeda, 'and they're far more romantic!'

He laughed, striking a match to light them.

'The trouble with you, Makeda,' he remarked, 'is that you don't mean half you say. Being romantic isn't a mood to light and snuff off again at the strike of a match.'

'I thought it was,' she countered, going round the table to light the wall-sconces. 'Soft lights and sweet music and a bottle of fine wine!' She lifted the bottle from the cooler where Mammy had placed it. 'What more could we want?'

'Nothing,' he assured her, 'except that time might stand still.' He came to put his arm about her. 'It's been running away from me far too fast these past two weeks,' he declared. 'I've loved working here, Makeda, and I'm glad there's more to do. I can imagine your father at Succoth working on the results of his expeditions, and it ties in so well with what

I know of him. He was a quiet man and he produced his results eventually. I never saw him in a hurry.'

'I wonder what he'd think of the progress we've already made,' Makeda mused, moving away from his encircling arm. 'It hasn't exactly been spectacular, but it has been thorough.'

'It's my idea of how it ought to be done.' He glanced at the clock in the far corner of the room, an old grandfather that had ticked away the seconds of her father's lifetime and her own. 'Shall we wait for Jacinthe or give Mammy a ring?'

'Jacinthe ought to be here by now. She knows what time it is,' Makeda decided. 'I'm starving, if you aren't! Jacinthe will come when she sees fit.'

Simon's understanding was something she had come to accept, she thought, and now she knew that she could rely on it. The warm way in which he spoke of her father's achievements wrapped her in a protective cloak which contrasted strongly with Grant's bleak condemnation of her unsophisticated approach to life. Perhaps she *was* a child at heart, but she was also adult enough to appreciate a man's approval now and then.

Simon set himself out to be pleasing, pouring the wine when Mammy had placed a casserole before them and lifted the lid with an expectant smile. The aroma of spiced chicken filled the air as the flickering candlelight lay reflected in the sparkling wine.

'A toast!' Simon proposed, lifting his glass. 'To our efforts in the future, Makeda! To a long co-operation in our chosen task!'

She raised her own glass, sipping the wine.

'I haven't any future beyond my father's book,' she said thoughtfully. 'It's a labour of love, if you like, Simon, something I have to do because he meant so much to me. It's—gratitude for his affection and the many sacrifices he made for us down through the years.'

She was more or less repeating Grant Ogilvie's words, acknowledging how true they were once she had thought deeply about them.

'It wouldn't be the same with anything else,' she added slowly. 'You have to give every ounce of your concentration to what you're doing and you have to respect and admire the person you are writing about.'

'Point taken!' he agreed. 'It wouldn't apply to me, would it? I've never really done anything worth while.'

'One day you will,' she assured him. 'And meanwhile, there's the book. I'll recognise your help, of course, with a note in the preface.'

'Thank you kindly,' he returned dryly.

'Oh, I'm sorry!' Makeda apologised. 'I didn't mean to sound patronising. You've worked hard—or will have done by the time we're finished, so you deserve a mention, at least.' She looked round as Mammy brought in the sweet. 'I'm surprised Jacinthe hasn't put in an appearance by this time,' she reflected.

'She am jus' come in,' Mammy informed her. 'My Ben say she was down at de village watchin' de boats. She am too often wanderin' on her own about de island.'

'I don't "wander", Mammy,' she said, 'and I reserve the right to be alone. You just tell Ben to mind his own business in future.' When she looked at Makeda her eyes were suddenly full of tears. 'I'm sorry if I'm late,' she added huskily. 'I had no idea of the time.'

'We've saved you an avocado pear and a helping of Mammy's spiced chicken,' Makeda said lightly, trying to ignore the tears. 'You must be as hungry as a hunter. Where have you been all day?'

'I've been to Crichton's, but now that Grant has the roof on and a door in place it's locked up. He'll do that with Succoth, I suppose, given time,' she added gloomily.

'He'll concentrate on Crichton's first,' said Makeda. 'We still have the lease on Succoth for as long as we need it.'

Jacinthe looked through the open jalousies to where Mammy had lit a single lamp on the verandah.

'It's all quite different,' she said, watching the night moths hovering in an ever-growing cloud. 'Everything about Succoth has changed.'

Simon poured some wine for her.

'Drink up!' he encouraged brightly. 'Things are never as bad as they seem just before the dawn! Did I tell you about a dig we made in Scotland once? We worked for two days excavating and hammering away until we unearthed the reference map someone had accidentally buried with his first few spadefuls only to discover that we were working in the wrong spot. The place we wanted was a couple of headlands away! The strange thing was that we found several good specimens where we were digging and not one in the listed site.'

'Jacinthe,' said Makeda, 'Simon and I thought of working for a couple of hours, but if you want to play Scrabble or something, we will.'

'Don't mind me,' Jacinthe said, digging into the avocado pear. 'I'll go to bed and read for a while.'

'You're sure?'

'Quite certain.' Jacinthe gazed down at her plate. 'Did you know they're going to have electricity at Crichton's?' she asked. 'Grant's bringing in a plant from Grenada, but he thinks there may be enough water in the lake to harness it eventually.'

'He *is* going to make a splash!' Simon observed. 'We'll be in radio communication with the mainland before he's satisfied.'

Jacinthe helped herself to a portion of Mammy's delicious chicken.

'He doesn't give much away,' she said, 'but he does seem eager to finish the work on Crichton's as quickly as possible.'

Simon led the way along the passage towards the study.

'What is Jacinthe going to be?' he asked.

'She isn't sure yet,' Makeda answered. 'Mother will help her decision along in the end. She believes everyone should have a career of some kind and I think, once Jacinthe has considered it, she'll become a nurse. She has always admired Abi.'

'She admires you all,' Simon reflected. 'You more than anyone, Makeda.'

'We're nearer an age,' Makeda explained, 'and when we were younger we had so many things in common. I suppose we ran wild on Millo, learning to swim and sail a boat and dive down to the coral long before it became a fashionable pursuit with people wearing masks and snorkels. Jacinthe could hold her breath longer than any of us and she could dive like a porpoise. She brought up all the shells and pieces of coral at the front of the house.'

'And she'll miss Millo like hell,' he rejoined. 'Ah, well, we can't always have things all our own way, as the snail said to the tortoise when the rabbit passed them! Look, are you sure you want to work at this hour of night? There's a new moon and a cool breeze blowing along the beach,' he tempted.

'We can look at the moon some other time,' Makeda decided, unlocking the desk drawer to take out the sheaf of papers which Simon had been busy with earlier in the day. It didn't look quite so bulky now that he had straightened out the sheets and stapled them together in batches for easier reference.

'Are you going to type?' he asked, settling himself at the table beside the window when he had lit both the lamps.

She nodded.

'I'd like to finish this chapter before we start on the notes,' she said. 'Will you flick through them again and let me know when they're ready?'

Her typewriting had once been a hit-and-miss sort of thing, but her recent concentration had improved it considerably. She had covered half a dozen pages in a very short space of time, bringing her to her goal at the end of the current chapter.

'That's it!' she said, leaning back in her chair to roll out the final sheet with a deep sense of achievement. 'Now for the notes, Simon, and another new beginning!'

There was no immediate answer from the other side of the room.

'Simon, are you still awake?' she joked, peering beyond the circle of lamplight on the table by the window.

Simon rose to his feet, standing by the table to look down at the papers spread out before him as if he had never seen them before, and she saw disbelief on his face and then overwhelming concern.

'Have you seen this?' he asked. 'There's a great hunk of paper here with nothing on it.'

'Nothing?' she repeated disbelievingly. 'There must be, unless it's been some sort of mistake.' She crossed quickly to his side. 'Knowing what he was like, Father could have left a few spare sheets in there while he ploughed on with the rest of his information.'

Simon met her eyes across the desk.

'There's no continuity,' he said. 'There are several pages missing, which means a lot of information we shall never know about. They could be crucial pages, and someone has substituted blank sheets. They've taken out what they wanted and left the rest for you to be going on with.'

'But, Simon,' she protested, her heart sinking lower with every unguarded word, 'no one else had access to the notes. You were the only one who looked at them——'

The flash of anger in his eyes silenced her before she went any further.

'I don't mean that you *took* them,' she hastened to apologise. 'I just meant——'

'What did you mean?' he demanded, his blue eyes suddenly hard. 'Don't accuse me too hastily, Makeda, for you could be wrong.'

'I know! I know that,' she cried, 'but I was just trying to say——'

'Yes?' Grimly he waited for her explanation. 'What were you going to say?'

She drew a quivering breath.

'That—someone must have taken them if they're not there. You say there's no continuity, nothing at all to show us what might have been in that section of the notes, so—so it looks quite deliberate, wouldn't you say?'

Her voice had steadied, but her thoughts were still whirling round in a maelstrom of distress. What was going to happen to her book, the one thing she could contribute to the memory of a beloved parent who had given her all the love and protection she had ever known?

'I can't believe it!' she cried. 'I don't want to believe it, Simon. No one could be so heartless as that. There must be some mistake!'

She clutched at the notes, her hands shaking as she flicked through them to the section of blank pages in the middle.

'The paper is almost the same,' she said. 'Whoever did this was trying quite deliberately to put us off the scent.'

'Or trying to make your work impossible,' Simon said carefully. 'It was someone who didn't want your book to be finished.'

'Grant?' Makeda's lips trembled on the name. 'It couldn't be!' she cried. 'He was never here, in this room, and the notes have never been out of my possession since I brought them from Barbados.'

'Which leaves me?' Simon suggested angrily. 'That's what you're thinking, isn't it? It was your first reaction when I told you a moment ago.'

'Simon, please!' she begged. 'I was too distressed to think straight. I know you couldn't—wouldn't have done such a thing.'

'All right,' he agreed, placated. 'The question now is, who did take them?'

'They came all the way from Saudi Arabia,' she said, 'among my father's belongings.'

'In a sealed package,' he pointed out. 'You told me so yourself.'

'Yes,' Makeda agreed, her heart turning over with disappointment. 'They must have been safe enough in the solicitors' hands.'

Simon paced the room, coming eventually to stand beside her.

'When you've put every other possibility out of your mind,' he said, 'you can come back to Grant Ogilvie.'

'No,' she said.

'He had every opportunity.' Simon's voice had hardened.

'He collected the notes from the lawyer's office in Bridgetown and delivered them to you several hours later.'

She nodded.

'What are you going to do?' he asked.

She could not answer him.

'The other notes Ogilvie offered you,' he persisted. 'They were his uncle's and possibly incomplete, so the information he needed must have been in here.' He flourished the sheaf of papers he had been working on the day before. 'Have you thought of that?'

'I can't think about anything, except that Grant didn't do it,' Makeda answered shakily. 'He would have come and asked for the information he wanted.' She hesitated, remembering that Grant had asked. He had suggested some kind of co-operation between them and when she had refused he had told her bluntly that he would publish from his uncle's notes without her help. She could not get away from the fact, and Simon was waiting for her answer. 'I'm going to bed,' she said rather desperately, 'and in the morning I'll go to Crichton's.'

'Do you want me to go with you?' he asked.

'No. I can manage this on my own.'

'I hope you can,' he said doubtfully. 'Ogilvie is a formidable character and you're still rather wet behind the ears. You need someone to stand up for you.'

She shook her head.

'Not any more, Simon,' she said. 'Once I would have rushed straight off to Crichton's and accused Grant out of hand for something he might not have done. I might even have waited for him coming off the trader after the dinner-party and created a scene right there on the beach, but it's all different now. I've got to think carefully, and the morning will be time enough for a showdown.'

'So long as you don't weaken,' he said.

'I won't!' She swallowed the lump that had gathered in her throat at the thought of Grant. 'I'm sorry our efforts have had to end like this. We were working so well together.'

'Too well, perhaps, from Ogilvie's point of view.' He

walked with her to the door. 'Are you sure you want to call it a day? It's still very early.'

'You'll understand,' she said. 'I have to think.'

He left her at the foot of the stairs, going off into the garden in search of Jacinthe. Makeda heard them talking on the verandah as she lay in bed with only a thin cotton sheet over her, and she wondered if Simon was telling Jacinthe why they had abandoned their plan to work for a couple of hours, discussing the theft with her. The word had an ugly connotation about it, but what else could she call it? Someone very close to Succoth had substituted ten blank sheets of foolscap for her father's original handwritten notes, and the people who had the greatest interest in the information contained in these pages were Grant, Simon and herself.

She lay thinking about Simon, eliminating every reason he could have had for such a substitution, and then, reluctantly, she thought about Grant and the motives he could have had.

Surely there was only one, the desire to publish the theories of the two professors before she had finished her father's book.

Her heart felt like lead as she turned and tossed in the warm bed. The room was full of starlight, not quite dark, and the tropic night spoke to her with a thousand voices. She could hear the waves lapping against the coral sand and the whisper of the coconut palms as they were stirred by a little night wind running through their ragged leaves, and long after midnight she heard the splash of oars and muted laughter as someone hauled a dinghy up the beach. Grant had come ashore with her mother and Heber and Dolly had thoroughly enjoyed the party.

Was Helen Rossiter with them?

Makeda jumped out of bed, standing in the shadows beyond the folded jalousies to watch. The three figures making their way up the beach were Dolly, Heber and Grant.

Several minutes after they had reached the verandah there was a chink of glass and her mother said, in a too-loud voice:

'We ought to have more little parties like this, Grant. Why don't you stay with us overnight? It would be much more comfortable than going back aboard your boat.'

Makeda held her breath, but what Grant answered in return was lost to her. The persistent little wind had soughed through the palm fronds at the wrong moment and if Grant had refused her mother's invitation she chose not to argue.

'Oh, well, that's fair enough,' she said, 'but I hope if you ever need anything in an emergency you'll come to Succoth.'

Makeda drew back from the window, lying down on her bed again. What was she going to say to Grant when she finally reached Crichton's? She would have to cross the Bluff early in order to catch him coming ashore from *Seafarer*, otherwise he would be working with the village men on the roof and she would have no chance to speak with him alone. She couldn't make a scene, as she might have done in the beginning, allowing her anger to get the better of her. She couldn't humiliate him in that way. 'One day you'll grow up, Sheba,' he had said. Was this what he had meant; stemming your pain and anger because you were in love?

Dawn was breaking before she finally fell into a troubled sleep and she was awake again by six o'clock. It would be after seven before Grant came ashore, perhaps even later than that if he had enjoyed the dinner-party aboard the trader, but she could not take the chance of missing him altogether.

Only Jacinthe saw her go. She had been standing at the window of her own room since daybreak, but she drew back involuntarily as Makeda took the narrow path up on to the Bluff. It joined the cleared road to Crichton's about a mile further on, but Makeda struck across the rougher ground towards the Bay.

Seafarer lay in the early-morning sunshine like a resting bird, rocking gently on the tide, but there was no movement aboard. The dinghy must be round the other side, she thought, since there was no sign of it on the beach. Then, after about half an hour, she saw Grant coming in across the reef. He had been fishing.

'Come aboard!' he yelled companionably. 'We can have a fry-up!'

He held aloft a string of fish, but she made no response to

his invitation, standing where he had first seen her at the far side of the bay. Almost immediately he sensed that something must be wrong.

'I'm coming ashore,' he called, slinging the fish aboard the yacht. 'Come down to the beach.'

She did as he asked, but she did not help him with the dinghy. Grant drew it well up on to the sand, fished under the stern seat for his deck shoes and came slowly towards her.

'What's wrong?' he demanded without any preliminary questioning. 'You look—upset.'

'Someone has stolen most of my father's notes.' Her eyes were compellingly green in the early-morning light. 'Whoever it was substituted blank foolscap for what must have been the most relevant part of the whole exercise.'

He took a step forward and she saw that his eyes were blazing.

'And you're not giving any prizes for the culprit's name?' His voice held an incisive note of contempt which cut sharply across her heart. 'You're quite sure who did it, aren't you? You came hot-foot across here at break of day to confront me with my perfidy. Good for you, Makeda! You make Sheba seem a very mild substitute for the kind of person you really are. I'm not guilty, but I'm not going to beg you to believe it. I don't work things out that way, but you might give a thought to the fact that I offered you my uncle's notes only a few days ago, so I've apparently changed my coat in a very short space of time.'

'When I refused to take them you were angry,' was all she could find to say.

'Certainly I was mad at you. I thought you cared about the book more than your foolish pride.' The anger was still dark in his eyes, but he did not touch her, although she had thought at first that he was about to shake her. 'When did you miss your father's notes?'

'Late last night. Simon and I decided to work on them after dinner and then we found that they'd been tampered with.'

128

His mouth clamped into a hard line.

'And so you came straight to me.'

'I'm not accusing you, Grant.'

'Then what is this? A vote of confidence, would you say?' His lip curled.

'I thought I might ask your advice.'

He laughed.

'What about? Did you expect me to play detective even though I'd substituted the blanks? I'm not like that at all, you know. If I've done a thing I'll say so.' He caught her by the shoulder. 'Just think! If I was so eager to be rid of you as you so fondly imagine, would I have taken the material you needed to get on with your work and so prolonged your stay at Succoth?'

She bit her lip, looking down at the sand.

'I hadn't thought of it like that,' she owned.

'Well, think now.' He freed her, turning his back on her to walk towards the dinghy. 'When you've come to another conclusion you can let me know.'

He rowed the distance between *Seafarer* and the shore with long, powerful strokes which seemed to accentuate his anger and disgust while Makeda stood watching, unable to think beyond the fact that she could have shared a pleasant breakfast of fried snapper, bread and marmalade with him in the freshness of the morning, sitting out on *Seafarer*'s deck with the murmur of the tide the only sound to be heard in all the lovely world of Millo, which she would never forget.

Going back to Succoth across the Bluff she realised that Grant hadn't offered her any easy solution to her dilemma. He hadn't even accused Simon, although he had once warned her indirectly about him. Obviously he didn't trust her father's erstwhile assistant, although somehow she felt that Simon was quite innocent of confiscating her father's notes. Without the previous batch, which was now part of her finished MS, they would be no real use to him.

No; she had to trust Simon in the same way that she trusted Grant, blindly, perhaps, but sincerely.

CHAPTER SEVEN

THE work at Crichton Place went on with a rapidity which was hard to believe. The weather was good and the men Grant brought in from Grenada worked with a will. Most of the time they were perched high on the roof, their brown bodies gleaming in the sun, the sound of their voices as they sang echoing across the bay. The music was pure calypso, with here and there an old plantation song creeping in to strike a proper balance and remind them that their real roots were close to the soil.

Makeda longed to go to Green Turtle Bay to look up at Crichton's with a roof on, but she could not bring herself to cross the Bluff, not because of a foolish sense of pride but because something inside her turned cold at the memory of Grant's anger. He had not acted like a guilty person, but he had walked away from her before she could apologise.

The fact that she could see Crichton Place from a distance took her often to the Bluff where she stood looking down at the activity in the other bay, hoping that no one would notice her. Grant took *Seafarer* to Grenada on several occasions, and each time she wondered if Helen Rossiter had returned with him, because Helen's interest in Crichton's would be two-fold. The restoration would be her first concern, satisfying her training as an architect, but over and above that she could be creating the background for her own future. As the prospective mistress of Crichton's, she would plan with Grant to make it the perfect home.

Then one day Makeda saw her. Helen was standing out on *Seafarer*'s deck in the same pair of blue trousers and blue shirt, although she had discarded the tomato-coloured waistcoat because of the heat. The ketch had come in the day before with more supplies, this time from Barbados, Heber had told them, although he had not mentioned Helen, which could have been an oversight on his part.

Makeda drew back a little way into the shadow of the scrub. There was no sign of Grant, but he could be below deck or even already on the job at Crichton's. Well, she couldn't let Helen see how desperately interested she was!

Plunging back across the Bluff, she met Simon coming up from Succoth with Jacinthe in tow.

'Were you thinking of working?' he asked. 'If so, I'll come back with you.'

They had agreed to go on with the MS up to the point where the blank pages had been substituted, hoping that something would transpire in the meantime to make it possible to finish the book.

'After that,' Makeda had declared unsteadily, 'I mean to go, whether it's up to publication standard or not. I can't go on accepting Grant's largesse for ever. When he's finished Crichton Place he'll want to start on Succoth so that he can bring in an estate manager or something of the kind.'

'I've half a notion he might offer the job to Heber,' Simon had said. 'He could go on being a geologist in his spare time.'

Heber and Grant had become close friends. They worked well together, with Heber chiselling away at the stonework and exploring the rock surfaces around the site. A giant mahogany tree had been felled just beyond the avenue to make room for some sort of extension and Makeda had been greatly intrigued, wondering what Grant planned to do there.

'We could work for an hour,' she told Simon. 'I've had my early-morning exercise up on the Bluff.'

'You go there a lot,' he observed. 'If you're so curious about Crichton Place why don't you go up there and ask to be shown round? It would be a perfectly normal request in the circumstances.'

Jacinthe looked at Makeda, her eyes sultry.

'She's afraid of Grant,' she said, 'and she doesn't trust him.'

'What absolute rubbish!' Makeda cried. 'I could go to Crichton's at any time.'

'Then why don't you?' her cousin challenged. 'I've been more than once and Grant had no objections.'

Because you have no part in the clash of wills which has set us apart, Makeda thought. Lucky Jacinthe!

Going back to Succoth with Simon she mentioned the fact that she had seen Helen Rossiter on *Seafarer*.

'She's part of the set-up, isn't she?' Simon mused. 'A very intelligent lady as well as being so beautiful. Do you think Ogilvie intends to marry her?'

'I don't know! I don't want to know,' Makeda declared. 'They're working together and he's evidently very—fond of her, so it could mean that they'll marry in the end. Possibly as soon as Crichton's is restored.'

'So that's the way it is?' Simon said cautiously. 'Are you going to Crichton's to take a look-see?' he asked after a moment. 'I'll go with you, if you like.'

'Not today.' Her lips were firm. 'Perhaps not ever.' She drew in a deep breath. 'Grant has no time for me, at Crichton's or anywhere else.'

'Because you bawled him out over the missing notes?'

'Not only that.'

'But you did tell him what you thought?'

'Not this time.'

'Makeda, you're slipping! If you believe he took them——'

'I don't.' She faced him squarely. 'They've gone and we may never discover where, or how they were taken, and we can't avoid the fact that we're working now in a sort of vacuum. We can't—daren't draw our own conclusions to finish the MS because we're writing about facts.'

'I'm with you a hundred per cent in that respect,' he agreed. 'It's just that it's such a damned waste having come this far only to have to give up a step before the end. All the evidence seems to be in these confiscated pages, and I could gnash my teeth at the thought of someone else having them and perhaps being able to use them to their own advantage.'

'They were my father's,' Makeda said with a catch in her

throat. 'They were something he cared deeply about, and now they've gone. Whoever has taken them will never know how badly I feel about their loss.'

Simon did not answer her. He seemed deep in protracted thought, and when they came to the end of the notes and faced the blank sheets of foolscap he laid down his pen with a sigh.

'I suppose this puts an end to my usefulness,' he observed. 'I can't tell you how sorry I am, Makeda, I've enjoyed working on Millo—working with you, I suppose I mean—but now I'll have to go.'

'There's no need for you to rush away,' Makeda said. 'My mother likes you and I'm sure you'll be welcome here till we go ourselves, if you want to stay so long.'

'Like you, I could be persuaded to stay for ever,' Simon assured her, 'but my lotus days are over now that we have very little hope of finishing the book. I must look for work, and since there's none to be had on Millo—not my kind of work, anyway—I must up anchor and sail away.'

'Not too soon,' said Makeda. 'You'll stay to see Crichton's finished, at least?'

He shook his head.

'I doubt if I could stay that long.' He seemed almost anxious to go now. 'I have a living to earn and I'm already deeply in your mother's debt.'

'She doesn't think so. She likes to be amused and she's become very fond of you.'

'The Court jester? Well, I can think of worse things to be,' he conceded. 'Before I go, though, I have to see how things are shaping up at Crichton's, then I won't have to tax my imagination in the future.' He came round behind her chair. 'Come with me,' he said. 'It's the sort of thing Ogilvie would expect.'

She was at a loss to understand his reference to Crichton's and the future.

'Perhaps tomorrow,' she said, not really wanting to go in case Grant would consider it trespassing after all she had said on the subject when they had first met.

Her mother declared that she could not allow Simon to 'escape' so easily. Dolly loved company and her husband's young ex-colleague had the happy knack of being amusing under any circumstances. She told Simon that he would be made welcome at Succoth for as long as he pleased, but now that he had apparently made up his mind, he was determined to go.

'I'l have another lotus week and then I might ask Ogilvie to take me over to Bridgetown,' he said.

He had never actually told Makeda that he was in love with her, and now even the little acts of affection were missing. He no longer put his arm about her or let his eyes dwell too long on her shadowed face, and when they walked in the garden together after dark they walked apart. Some of the magic had gone out of the island for Simon, too.

The following morning Helen Rossiter came over the Bluff, walking down across the beach to stand for a while at the jetty, looking out to sea. Then she came swiftly up the overgrown path to Succoth and knocked on the inside door. The screen had been left open because a brisk wind had blown away all the flies, and Mammy hurried through from the kitchen at the unexpected summons.

'Oh, sure, Miss Rossiter, ma'am,' Makeda heard the Carib woman saying. 'Yo' jus' come right in an' I go get Miss Garland right away.'

'Will I do?' Makeda asked, crossing the hall to meet their visitor. 'My mother is still in the shower.'

'I've come too early,' Helen regretted, 'but it's cooler walking at this time of day.'

'Will you come in?' Makeda asked. 'Or could I bring you something to drink on the verandah?'

'I'd like that,' said Helen, seating herself on the nearest lounger. 'It's not that I dislike walking—I do a lot of it in my job—but the going isn't exactly easy on the headland, is it?'

'Not if you're not used to it,' Makeda allowed, feeling suddenly young and gauche in such sophisticated company.

'I'll go and get the drinks. Would a fruit punch be all right? I've just been preparing the paw-paw.'

'I can't think of anything I would like better,' Helen smiled.

Makeda glanced in the mirror as she went through the hall, thinking how like a scarecrow she looked in her blue-and-white gingham blouse and shabby jeans with her hair caught in two short bunches behind her ears to keep it from falling over her face as she worked. Her arms and neck were as brown as mahogany and her bare feet were thrust into a pair of ancient deck shoes which had lost their toe-caps. Now that there was no book to take up her attention she helped Mammy in the kitchen, and perhaps that was where she truly belonged.

I've got a fit of the 'Poor Makedas', she thought, measuring paw-paw into two tall glasses, and the only way to deal with that is to snap out of it!

'What she want?' Mammy asked, nodding towards the verandah. 'She comin' here to stay?'

'Not that I know of, Mammy.' Makeda paused at the kitchen door. 'What put that idea into your head?'

'Miss Garland, she say she come if she like,' Mammy reminded her. 'But then Miss Rossiter, she go to that ol' boat in Green Turtle an' we forget about it.'

'Perhaps *Seafarer* is going away for a while,' Makeda said. 'That could be the answer.'

Slowly she returned to the verandah, carrying the tray with the two glasses on it. Helen got up to help with the tray, moving a second lounger nearer to the table.

'Have you been over to Crichton's yet?' she asked when Makeda sat down. 'We're getting on like a house on fire. It's amazing what a bit of enthusiasm can do. The roof's finished now and we're working inside. It's interesting to see it at every stage of the restoration, I think. Why not come back with me?'

But Makeda could not go to Crichton's unless Grant invited her.

'I'll see it when it's finished,' she decided, releasing ⊦

cloud of auburn hair from the confining elastic bands. 'I know it will be just as you want it.'

'I've worked with Grant before.' Helen sipped the punch. 'This is wonderful, Makeda! Is it your own recipe? Mostly my efforts have gone into the decorating of Grant's hotels, but it's much more fun working from the ground up—or the roof down, to be more accurate!' Her laughter was like the breaking of the little waves on the beach. 'Grant is so easy to please and he leaves me to my own devices, which is most satisfying to my ego.'

'Are you going to plan everything?' Makeda asked.

'Right down to the final cup and saucer, unless Grant changes his mind and brings in someone else for the final details. Soft furnishings is something I'm not very keen on, anyway. I prefer to get right down to basics. A lot of good furniture is essential, of course, and Grant plans to have it sent in from Barbados. He's off there in the morning, which is the main reason for my visit,' she added. 'I've been keeping him from his comfortable bunk on board *Seafarer*, although I must say he's been more than kind about it. Secretly I think he enjoyed his Boy Scout existence at Crichton's,' she smiled. 'He says it's years since he lived rough under canvas and it's done him a lot of good.'

It was impossible not to warm to this amazing person who held both Grant's respect and affection. Helen was so natural, so utterly free from airs and graces, that Makeda capitulated almost immediately.

'I'm sure my mother's invitation still stands,' she said. 'She loves young company.'

'It was so kind of her to offer me a bed if I ever needed one,' Helen said. 'I could have borrowed the tent, but Grant was rather against the idea, and to sail to and fro each time *Seafarer* goes to Barbados isn't my idea of getting on with the job.'

'How long do you expect it to take?' Makeda asked, wondering if everything would be finished before they had to leave the island.

'Not long. The walls are in excellent condition and, of

course, the foundations are very good. Crichton's was built on a rock, and no mistake! That's why I'm so glad that Grant has decided to restore it for his own use.'

Dolly came to the open window of the dining-room, stepping out to join them.

'Helen!' she exclaimed. 'How nice to see you. Has Makeda been taking good care of you?' She looked like a young girl in her flowered *peignoir* with her fair hair hanging down her back and eyes alight with interest. 'I hope you've come to stay.'

'I've come to ask for a roof over my head for a night or two,' Helen confessed. 'If it's a great inconvenience, of course, you must tell me.'

'Your bed is already made up,' Dolly said. 'When I thought of you sleeping on that dreadful yacht I felt quite guilty.'

'There was no need,' Helen told her. '*Seafarer* is very well equipped and Grant's bunk was so comfortable I had trouble getting up in the mornings. Seriously, though,' she added, 'I want to work as hard as possible while Grant is away. I've another job waiting to be done and I've more or less promised to be finished here by the end of the month.'

'And then we'll lose you?' Dolly suggested.

'Oh, no!' Helen laughed. 'I'll be coming back. Millo has its own particular fascination, and Crichton's is partly my brain-child, you know. I bullied Grant into it, I'm afraid, but I don't think he regrets it now.'

Makeda left them together to make their plans.

'It will be so nice to have Helen with us,' Dolly said later in the day. 'And even when Grant comes back with *Seafarer* I think she ought to stay here. Makeda,' she added, 'have you made any other arrangements to finish your father's book? Simon told me about the notes and I really can't think who could have taken them. Were they very, very valuable?'

'They were essential to what I wanted to do,' Makeda answered.

'And you just couldn't go ahead without them?'

'Not very well.' Makeda hesitated. 'I couldn't use my

imagination, for one thing. It's not that kind of book. I have to know the absolute facts.'

'I see.' Dolly sighed. 'I wonder where all this leaves us now. We'll have to go, of course, but I must confess I was rather counting on the book to help out financially until your father's affairs are finally settled. The contract Professor Hunt made with him about Succoth will end immediately, I suppose.'

'I shall have to tell Grant that I've tried and failed, and that we'll go.'

Dolly hesitated, knowing how much Millo had always meant to her.

'I really don't see how you could stay here anyway, my dear,' she pointed out with genuine sympathy. 'Heber has to go back to college and I must see to Jacinthe's future education. Can you believe it, she wants to be a nurse? Following in Abi's footsteps, I suppose. It's only you who are so deeply involved.'

'I know.' Restlessly Makeda paced about the room. 'I'm aware of what's at stake, but I wish I hadn't failed Father so dismally. This book was something he wanted to do. It was part of him.'

'I'm afraid so,' Dolly agreed, not yet being able to understand. 'You had a great deal of privacy here to write and Simon was a tremendous help to you, but now he says he must go and there's really very little you can do in the circumstances.'

Makeda stood beside the window for several minutes without speaking, looking out across the verandah to the ragged patch of banana trees growing between the house and the scrub. Her father had planted them several years ago and they had not been properly cultivated, but they still produced a reasonable crop of small, sweet bananas which were pleasant to eat. Her thoughts were far away from the Succoth garden, however, as she looked up towards the Bluff.

'There's something I could do,' she said carefully, as if she had come to the conclusion after a great deal of tortuous thought. 'I could sink my pride and go to see Grant. I could ask him for the use of his uncle's notes.'

'Would that be quite the same thing?' Dolly asked doubtfully.

'I don't know. It could be the answer and, again, they could be quite useless. No two people think exactly alike, but if both sets of notes related to an actual find then they *would* be useful.'

Dolly could see her personal freedom receding a little farther into the future.

'Are you sure Grant would wish you to have them?' she asked.

'He's offered them to me twice in the past few weeks and I've been too pig-headed to accept his help.' Makeda came to stand beside the table.

'Certainly you were always rather stubborn,' Dolly agreed. 'Once you'd made up your mind it was difficult to convince you otherwise, but if you're sure you want to approach Grant——'

'I don't *want* to, but I must,' said Makeda. 'I may feel— humiliated going cap-in-hand to him, but that will be a small price to pay if I can finish the book in time.'

'I can't see any reason why Grant should refuse you,' Dolly reflected. 'Helen says he's amazingly kind.'

'Perhaps Helen hasn't rubbed him up the wrong way.' Makeda turned to the door. 'I have, and I wouldn't be at all surprised if he turned me down flat.'

'You can only ask,' Dolly said. 'Helen expects him back the day after tomorrow.'

She had two whole days to reconsider her decision, Makeda thought, but already she knew that she would not go back on it now.

'If you get Professor Hunt's notes will you ask Simon to stay on and help?' Dolly asked.

'If he will.' Makeda had almost forgotten about Simon's resolve to find another job elsewhere. 'He was very easy to work with.'

'He has to make a living,' Dolly conceded. 'He's not a very wealthy young man.'

'I had thought of offering him a part share in the book,' Makeda mentioned. 'I was going to ask you what you thought about it, since the royalties will come to you.'

'Oh, dear me!' Dolly exclaimed. 'After all the work you've put in on it?'

'Don't let's quibble about it, Mother.' Makeda had turned in the doorway, smiling a little. 'You can call it a labour of love, if you like. That will make it all sound very grand as far as I'm concerned!'

'You *are* a strange girl,' Dolly accused her, 'but I suppose you know best what you want to do.'

The thought of going to Grant to reverse her former blunt refusal was in the forefront of Makeda's mind for the next two days, and when Helen mentioned that *Seafarer* had returned with a load of material from Barbados she climbed over the Bluff early the following morning to catch him as he came ashore.

She found the yacht's dinghy pulled up on the beach, but Grant himself was nowhere to be seen.

It means Crichton's, she thought, realising that she hadn't taken a first visit to his future home into account when she had set out so resolutely to make her request. In for a penny, in for a pound, she decided, climbing the narrow pathway from the shore which eventually led to the avenue of mahogany trees. He can but turn me away empty-handed.

Nevertheless, her heart was pounding by the time she eventually reached the shelter of the trees. Crichton Place had been magnificent in its day, with an uninterrupted view over Green Turtle Bay to the wide stretch of the Caribbean lying in the sun. Up here the outline of Pelican Island showed faintly beyond the reef, while the darker Dutchman's Cap drifted on the tide like the discarded headgear it so closely resembled.

Grant had made a tremendous difference everywhere, clearing away rubble and fallen masonry as he had discarded it so that the house stood out clearly on its elevated site as it must have done when it was newly-built by David Crichton all these years ago. It was a pity, Makeda thought, that such a well-respected man should have produced such a tyrannical son, but legends were odd things and perhaps Samuel Crichton had not been as bad as he was painted.

There was a great deal of activity at the house itself, with the native workers already on the scene and the few inevitable onlookers who had come to criticise standing around with their sisal hats pulled down over their eyes and a handy straw between their decaying teeth. Heber, who was in charge of the workforce, had not yet put in an appearance, but the village men were already busy with the tasks assigned to them the evening before.

She saw Grant, at last, standing on the threshold of his future home, and somehow he seemed larger than life in that moment, the plantation overlord worthy both of Crichton's and Millo because he belonged there. He stood under the great colonnaded porch waiting for her to reach him, the surprise he felt openly mirrored in his eyes.

Before he could make any mocking reference to her hasty visit, she said quickly:

'I tried to catch you down on the beach. I didn't mean to come to Crichton's uninvited, but you do start early and—and there's something I have to ask you.'

It had sounded absurdly young and breathless, but she had not been able to think of anything else to say.

'So it wasn't just curiosity that brought you?' He was half-smiling as he looked down into her flushed face. 'I wondered when you would come.'

'I was going to wait till I was asked,' Makeda tried to say with dignity. 'After all, this is your home now and I have no right to intrude.'

'Is that what you call it?' He turned to the open door behind him. 'Will you come in?' he asked. 'Since we're being so conventional.'

Makeda hesitated.

'What are you afraid of, Sheba?' he smiled. 'The days of Samuel Crichton are long since past.'

'I—always felt that Samuel was slightly overdone,' she said, pulling up before the magnificent inner door which had now replaced the temporary slatted one. 'It's magnificent!' she cried. 'You've had it made from the local mahogany.'

'There was plenty of felled timber lying around, nicely weathered for the purpose,' he said. 'None of it has been wasted, as a matter of fact. We're using the rest for panelling. What do you think of the carving?' He ran his fingers over the lower section of the door. 'Old Joe Cartoga did it. He's a wonderful craftsman.'

'Everything is perfect.' There was an odd, hard lump at the back of her throat as they entered the lofty hall. 'All those magnificent beams showing on the ceiling must have been how Crichton's looked in the beginning.'

'We're working from the original plans. Fortunately they weren't destroyed and I was able to have them.' He led her through the empty hall to an equally empty room at the rear of the house. 'When it's finally completed I think I should feel satisfied. I couldn't have done it without Helen, of course,' he added. 'She has the know-how and an awful lot of enthusiasm.'

'Grant,' she said because suddenly she could not bear to think of Helen here at Crichton's as his wife, 'I've come to ask you to let me have your uncle's notes, after all. I deserve to be refused,' she rushed on, 'but if you would only consider it I would be extremely grateful.'

He turned to face her in the revealing early-morning light.

'Don't look so humble, Sheba,' he said. 'I know exactly how you feel. You can have the notes with my blessing and I won't even point out that I offered them to you some time ago.'

'You mean that?'

He took her arm.

'Of course I mean it. I'm not given to making promises and then going back on my word.'

'I realise that,' she acknowledged humbly.

'Come and see the rest of the house,' he invited, 'and then we can row over to *Seafarer* and pick up the notes.'

She followed him down the long hall to where a branched staircase led to the upper floor. Although Crichton's had been virtually without a roof for many years, very little had been pilfered, which might have been due to the fear engendered by the legend and the reputation of Samuel Crichton. A 'haunt' was a very serious thing on the island and Grant had been able to restore the staircase in a very short space of time. The upper floor had been extensively damaged by water, but it was almost dried out now, the musty smell which goes with all neglected property scarcely noticeable.

'Ten bedrooms,' Grant mused. 'David Crichton evidently built for a rapidly-growing family. The oldest son always moved into Succoth when he married, of course, and came back to Crichton Place when he finally inherited the plantation.'

'Was Samuel an only son?' Makeda asked.

'Apparently. Hence the fierce reputation, I suppose. He was probably spoiled from infancy. Most of the work we still have to do is up here,' he went on to explain, throwing open the repaired double doors at the head of the staircase. 'I gather this was the master suite since the windows look down on most of the island.'

He crossed the bare floor, waiting for Makeda to follow him. A large four-poster bed stood against one wall, a relic of past magnificence which Makeda remembered from childhood forays to Crichton's, but otherwise the room was empty.

'Samuel was probably born in that bed,' Grant reflected. 'It went with the house along with a few other things which were too heavy or not attractive enough to ship out to the mainland. As a family, the Crichtons just seemed to disintegrate, with only a very old woman left to tell the tale of former grandeur in the end. She leased Millo. She leased Millo to an outsider before she died because there was no male heir to inherit.'

'And my father sold out to your uncle,' said Makeda. 'Crichton's has had a checkered history.' She touched the ornate carving on the massive headboard. 'I remember weaving all sorts of fantastic tales about this bed,' she confessed. 'The carvings alone were enough to frighten the lives out of us when we were younger. All those masks on the prows of the ships were easily identified with the legend, but I could never reconcile the flowers. They are beautiful, aren't they?'

She had forgotten why she had come now that the ice was broken between them and she had made her request. Grant had responded immediately, teasing her only a little, and now he was revealing his pride in Crichton's with the knowledge that she would understand.

'I have something which really belongs here,' she confessed. 'I took it away because I couldn't bear to see anything so beautiful being spoiled by the damp. It's a wooden box—not very big—but all inlaid with mother-of-pearl, a lady's sewing box, perhaps, because it has little trays inside and a padded lid. It was quite empty, but I suppose I *did* steal it. Somehow I never thought of Crichton's being restored and the box seemed a very small thing to take, but I'll bring it back, or—or I could give it to Helen.'

He laughed at her obvious concern.

'Since it's so small a thing, Sheba, let me make you a present of it,' he offered lightly. 'There would be very little point in bringing it back to an empty house.'

'Thank you very much.'

She stood gazing at the carved masks on the bed headboard, picturing the room as it had once been, while Grant watched her out of the corner of his eye.

'This must be the finest view on the whole island,' he remarked, 'but you're no doubt aware of that when you came here so often in your younger days to steal sewing-boxes.'

Makeda smiled.

'Before the glass was finally blown out we used to clean spy-holes in the window-panes to watch for approaching pirate ships,' she confessed. 'We imagined them down there in the bay where *Seafarer* is now.'

'All respectable pirates come with a diesel engine in their bilges these days,' Grant laughed. 'You certainly don't give in, Sheba, do you?'

'I don't want to argue any more,' she said. 'You've been more than generous about your uncle's notes.'

'I'm quite sure you'll make good use of them,' he said. 'It would have been some considerable time before I could have got down to the job. I felt that Crichton's should come first, you see.'

She lingered for a moment at the double doors, trying to imagine what the room would look like when Helen had furnished it. There was another, smaller room, leading off to the right, which was the master's dressing-room, and Jo Cartoga was already at work on the panelling. Very soon it would all be ready for the new master of Crichton's and the woman who would be his wife.

'There's very little more to see,' said Grant. 'I expect you know the lie of the land downstairs as well as I do. We're modernising the kitchens, but Helen will show you all that when the work is complete.'

'Yes.'

Makeda's voice was no more than a whisper as she preceded him downstairs. These few intimate moments in the room above had meant nothing to him, while she would cherish them for ever, like the fool she was!

Heber was coming along the road from Succoth when they reached the open air and he seemed surprised to see her.

'We're going on board *Seafarer*,' Grant announced. 'I'll be back within half an hour to help with the bulldozer.'

A small J.C.B. had been brought in by the trader to clear the scrub, and they were dealing with the undergrowth in half the time it would have taken to do the job by hand. Heber nodded his acknowledgement of Grant's promise, still slightly puzzled by his sister's early-morning call, but Makeda didn't stop to enlighten him. Helen would probably tell him all about her errand, anyway, once she had heard it from Grant.

They walked down to the beach, running the dinghy into the shallow green water.

'Hop aboard,' said Grant. 'You can row, if you have a mind to,' he told her in the tone he would have used to an eager urchin who was mad about the sea.

Makeda took the oars, waiting till he had pushed off and clambered into the stern, his brown limbs dripping water as he stretched them out on either side of her own.

'Green Turtle is the perfect hideaway,' he observed, looking across the bay. 'No wonder so many seafaring gentlemen preferred it to Frenchman's once they'd worked out how impregnable it was inside the reef.'

'Once you know the passage,' Makeda agreed, 'it's an ideal little anchorage, but in a bad wind it can be dangerous because of the coral.'

'I've a lot to learn,' he said without rancour. 'Green Turtle has become a sort of challenge as far as I'm concerned.'

She brought the dinghy alongside the ketch.

'Are you coming on board?' he asked.

'You told Heber you would be straight back,' she reminded him.

'Which just leaves us time for a drink,' he decided. 'Up you go!' He held the dinghy steady with a hand on *Seafarer*'s rail. 'I may have to look for the notes, although I know they're on board.'

'Have you been through them?' she asked eagerly, feeling that this was at least something they might have in common.

He shook his head.

'They're still in the lawyer's sealed packages, so you can rest assured there's no hanky-panky attached to my offer.'

Makeda climbed aboard, remembering her first visit to the ketch when she had swum through the clear water of the bay to look in at the porthole on the afterdeck.

'What is it to be?' Grant asked, standing in the galley doorway. 'Coke, or lime, or both?'

'Lime-juice will be fine,' she told him. 'I've got an enormous thirst to quench!'

They sat out on deck when Grant had poured the drinks, letting the sun seep into their bodies with a blessed disregard of time.

'If this is what's known as "going native",' Grant mused, 'I'm all for it!'

'Yet you don't really waste time,' she said. 'You're about the busiest person I know. Look at what you've done with Crichton's in little more than a month.'

'A labour of love is something quite different, as you ought to know,' he said. 'It's hardly "work" in the true sense of the word.'

A labour of love! Her heart turned over as she looked at him sprawled beside her on the warm deck, obviously content. That was exactly what his present activities were all about. He had taken time off from his more serious work to make himself a home. Like Solomon of old, he was about to recompense himself for all the hard work he had put in on the building of an empire, relying on Helen to make his dream come true.

She sat upright, draining her glass.

'If I can have the notes I'll make myself scarce and let you get on with Crichton's,' she said. 'Could I come and see it when it's finished, Grant? Before you finally move in, I mean.'

He smiled at the impulsive request.

'I'll be giving a party,' he said. 'Helen considers it absolutely necessary to have a sort of mock Crop Over after we've put in all the hard effort, and I expect she'll be looking to you for some help.'

How could she help his future wife with the festivities to come, yet how could she possibly refuse?

Grant went in search of the notes while she sat on the sun-warmed deck, thinking about the future.

'I don't know why I'm doing this,' he said when he returned with the sealed package in his hand.

'You could have used them yourself,' she suggested.

'No chance! They're only half the story, I suspect, and I had no real right to them.'

He took the oars on the way back to the beach.

'How long do you think it will take you to finish the book?' he asked.

'About a month. After that,' she added slowly, 'Succoth will be yours.'

'I've no immediate need for it,' he said as she helped him to draw the dinghy up the beach.

'Don't thank me again,' he said as they parted. 'Just make a good job of the MS for your father's sake. Heber tells me that Wetherby is on his way out,' he added tentatively, 'but this may make a difference.'

Makeda hesitated.

'I think it does,' she said. 'I mean to ask Simon to stay.'

He watched her go across the sand and he was still standing beside the dinghy when she began to climb up the Bluff, a heavy frown etching two dark furrows between his brows.

CHAPTER EIGHT

SIMON took quite a bit of persuasion when Makeda asked him to stay for at least another two weeks to help finish the MS. She had no idea what George Hunt's notes would contain, although she hoped that there would be something important in them.

Dolly, when she heard of the change of plans, added her persuasion to Makeda's.

'You couldn't be more welcome,' she assured Simon when they discussed it. 'We were all going to miss you terribly when you went away.'

Makeda decided that it was time to offer Simon a share in the finished book.

'No,' he said emphatically. 'I couldn't accept that sort of gesture. Give me a mention, if you like, but filthy lucre—no! Have you thought that it might not earn so very much, anyway?'

'It's not important,' Makeda said. 'It was just that I wanted you to have a fair share.'

He moved his chair nearer to hers, as if he wanted to say something of importance, then he lay back against the stiff headrest and looked up at the sky.

'Shares, whether fair or otherwise, were never my cup of tea, Makeda,' he declared. 'I always had to own the whole caboodle or nothing at all. When I first came out here I thought I would write my own book from the few facts I possessed, but when I started to work with you I knew how futile that was. I had no real standing, for one thing, and I couldn't write. I would have needed your help, and I thought the best way to get it was to make love to you.'

She looked aghast at his confession.

'It didn't work, did it?' he observed whimsically. 'Not while Ogilvie had such a head start.'

'Oh, Simon!' She hid her face in her hands. 'You must know it isn't any use. He's going to marry Helen and live at Crichton's. That's what the rush to finish the restoration is all about.'

'You surprise me,' Simon said. 'You surprise me greatly. Helen isn't a widow, you know. She has a husband tucked away somewhere—in London, I think.'

'It can't be true,' Makeda whispered. 'I can't believe it. She's such a nice person.'

'Even nice people can have an unhappy love affair,' he reminded her. 'Look at me!'

'Simon, I'm sorry!' she cried. 'I thought we were just having a harmless flirtation.'

'No flirtation is truly harmless,' he pointed out morosely. 'Someone is nearly always bound to be hurt. But we're getting far too morbid,' he added. 'Tell me about your early-morning visit to Crichton's and your trip out to *Seafarer*.'

She held up the sealed package which Grant had given her the day before.

'His uncle's notes were on the ketch, but Grant had never had time to open them.' She had avoided any further mention of Crichton's. 'I suppose he meant to look at them one day, but he has so many other things to see to—more important things. Anyway, he passed them over with no strings attached.'

Simon opened one eye.

'Did you expect strings?'

'I thought he might set a time limit,' she confessed.

'He can't want Succoth that badly,' Simon said. 'If he's waiting for Helen's divorce to come through it could be months yet before they were able to marry. Oh, I'm sorry!' He got hastily to his feet. 'I didn't mean to be so clumsy, Makeda. Forgive me!'

'You weren't,' she told him. 'It's just that I haven't got used to the idea yet. Simon, I've a feeling that I've got to get away,' she confessed unhappily. 'I've got to put some sort of limit to my life here on Millo, although it's the last thing I would have considered a couple of months ago.'

'We'll finish the book first,' he said, taking her arm to walk her along the beach. 'When would you like to start?'

'Tomorrow,' she decided. 'We'll open up the package in the morning and start to work.'

Helen came back from Green Turtle Bay earlier than usual that afternoon. The trader had come in at four o'clock and Simon had gone down for the mail. There was quite a bundle of letters, most of them for Grant, but as Simon flicked through the envelopes at the verandah table Helen seemed to be waiting for some sort of personal communication.

'Mrs Rossiter.' Simon tossed an envelope into her lap. 'All the way from London, would you believe?'

Helen smiled at him, the slow, careful smile that had won all their hearts, but Makeda's own heart seemed to stand still as she waited for Helen to open the letter. The address was typewritten, scored out, and re-addressed to Millo.

Simon moved uneasily to the far side of the table, but Helen made no effort at privacy as she tore back the flap and took out a single sheet of writing-paper.

'Excuse me,' she murmured. 'This may be important.'

Makeda gathered up the family mail to carry it into the house while Simon went off to Crichton's with the remainder. At the dining-room doorway she turned. There had been no actual sound from the still figure on the cane lounger, but it didn't take much imagination to see how deeply Helen was affected by what she had just read.

'What is it?' Makeda asked impulsively. 'Can I do anything to help?'

Helen shook her head.

'We never really expect it when it comes,' she said with a far-away look in her eyes. 'Makeda, I must go back with the trader. My husband is dying.'

'Oh—I'm sorry!' The words were not entirely conventional. 'I had no idea,' Makeda said.

'He's been ill for so long,' said Helen. 'Too ill even to

recognise us. Eight years of suffering is too much. He was such a patient man, Makeda, but this past year he's looked so weary. I would never have come away like this if I'd known how near the end he really was, but I have to work. I have a son at an English public school and a daughter in a French convent. We're so scattered, but it's the way it had to be, the way Desmond wanted it.'

'He—may get well,' Makeda attempted to comfort her, while she knew how futile it was.

Helen shook her head.

'They would never have sent for me if it wasn't serious. I spend as much time as I can at the nursing home, but they know my work takes me abroad a lot.'

'The trader goes out again on the next tide,' Makeda reminded her. 'Shall I fetch Grant for you?'

'There's no need.' Helen got to her feet. 'It would only upset him to see me so distressed. Desmond was his friend, but I don't want Grant to drop everything and rush off to London with me. He knows how much in love Desmond and I were; he knows I'll want to be alone with him at the end.'

'You'll come back?' Makeda asked.

'One day.'

After the trader had sailed away Makeda wondered if she should have disregarded Helen's wishes and sent for Grant, but it was too late for regret.

It seemed, however, that Grant did not intend to follow Helen to England.

'She wants to be alone,' he said when Heber carried the news to Crichton's the following morning, 'and I have to respect her wishes. Helen's the sort of person who wouldn't say a thing like that unless she meant it. We've discussed it all before, as a matter of fact, just in case this happened when she was away from England. I don't feel guilty about asking her to come to Millo,' he added. 'She needed the work. These two children of hers are her entire world and nothing but the best is good enough for them. They're Desmond's children, and that's how it is.'

It was something they had to accept, but Grant stopped work early that afternoon and climbed right out to Morgan's Reach on the north side of the island, not returning till after dark.

The following morning Simon came to waken Makeda. She hadn't slept until dawn and had then fallen into an uneasy doze from which she wakened with a start at the sound of his voice.

'"Lazybones, sleepin' in the sun",' he chanted. 'Do we work this morning or not?'

'We work,' she agreed, swinging her legs over the edge of the bed. 'Have you had your breakfast?'

'Hours ago!' he lied. 'Even your mother is up.'

'What about Jacinthe?'

'She's gone to Crichton's.'

'Crichton's? In lieu of Helen, do you mean?'

'Something like that. Do you want one of Mammy's stuffed eggs or just fruit?'

'Fruit will do. It's too hot for anything else. I think we're in for a storm.'

'I'm allergic to thunder and lightning,' Simon groaned.

'Wait till you've lived through a real live hurricane! Winds of a hundred and fifty miles an hour and the sea in the back garden!'

'Don't try to scare me! Have you?'

'Have I what?'

'Lived through a real live hurricane?'

'I must have done, since I'm still here.' Makeda padded out to the verandah in her bare feet, feeling the warmth of the floorboards under her toes. 'There was a terrible blow a while back. It took the roof right off Crichton's, but it missed Succoth entirely. Blows are like that—selective!'

'I'm going to start work,' Simon said. 'I don't want to hear any more.'

She grinned after his retreating figure, biting into a pawpaw. Simon wasn't the sort of person to survive life in the Islands.

Her mother came to join her, wearing her flowered peignoir.

'I thought I heard Simon,' she said.

'He was here a moment ago, but he's beaten me to it. We're going to work,' Makeda explained.

'It's really far too hot.' Dolly pushed the damp hair off her forehead. 'I'm sure it isn't as warm as this in Bridge-town.'

'Warmer,' Makeda declared unsympathetically. 'Have you had your shower?'

'Certainly I've had my shower!' Dolly was indignant. 'It's the first effort I make when I get up.'

'How about a swim?' Makeda rose from the table. 'It's heavenly in the cove first thing in the morning.'

'No, thank you!' said Dolly.

Simon was waiting in the study doorway.

'What is it?' Makeda asked urgently. 'You look ghastly.'

'That's exactly how I feel,' he agreed, turning back into the room. 'I've been through George Hunt's notes and they're an exact duplication of your father's—the ones you worked on together to write the first half of the MS. On the face of it, they're absolutely useless.'

'Oh, Simon!' The terrible disappointment of his revelation struck Makeda like a physical blow. 'I can't believe it. I just can't!'

'It's unfortunately true,' Simon said. 'You only have to look at the first few pages to be absolutely sure. It's rotten luck—for both of us, I guess.'

Quick tears gathered in Makeda's eyes, tears of frustration and hopelessness which she had crushed back so deter-minedly when her father's notes had disappeared.

'Even Grant couldn't help,' she said. 'Maybe there's some sort of hoodoo on the dig, a curse or something.'

Simon put a comforting arm about her shoulders.

'You know you don't believe that,' he said gently. 'What was it you said about the haunt up at Crichton's?'

'I said the natives believed in it, but I didn't. Well, not entirely!'

'You can't qualify a thing like that.'

'Well then, I don't really believe in a curse or anything like that.' She dried her eyes. 'It's just that—this was something I wanted to do so much. I wanted to finish my father's book because it was all I could do for him. It was to be a sort of memorial to his memory.' Her voice shook. 'Now it will never be finished.'

A movement outside the open window made them turn, but the jalousies were half closed to keep out the sun and by the time Simon had opened them the garden was deserted.

'I'm sure there was someone out there,' Simon said, frowning.

'It would be Mammy, or maybe Jacinthe going to gather the eggs.' Makeda was tying up the bundle of notes Grant had given her on *Seafarer*. 'I'll have to return them right away,' she decided.

'I wish there was something I could do,' said Simon.

'There isn't. You've done all you can, and so have I.' Her voice was quite steady now. 'We must give Grant a definite date for vacating Succoth so that he can continue straight on with the work he plans to do here when he's finished Crichton's. I'll speak to Mother this afternoon.'

The following morning she went to Crichton's with their decision fully made. Dolly hadn't been unduly averse to leaving the island at the end of the month to travel back to Barbados with Heber, and Jacinthe, as usual, hadn't voiced any opinion on the matter. She had accepted their joint decision in the way she did most things these days, in a remote sort of silence which nobody was able to penetrate. Heber had tried more than once to put their relationship back on to the old brother–sister basis and Simon joked with her as often as he could, but it all seemed to be to no avail.

Crichton's was a hive of industry when Makeda reached Green Turtle Bay and she stood for a moment listening to the clang of a hammer on stone and the whine of a power-saw as it cut through an unwanted tree. Another mahogany, perhaps, which was in the way of Grant's swift progress and could be put to better use to augment the panelling inside the house in a few years' time when it was fully matured.

Grant was nowhere to be seen, and for a moment she thought that he must have gone in search of Helen, but *Seafarer* was still anchored in the bay and there was no other way he could have left the island.

She climbed the path from the beach on to the avenue, and suddenly the whine of the saw ceased and Grant strode out of the undergrowth to confront her.

Evidently surprised by her early-morning call, he put down the saw and came towards her, standing in the slant of sunlight penetrating the trees. Stripped to the waist, with a red sweat bandana about his throat, he looked larger than life all of a sudden, a man above the average finding a zest in the tasks of the primitive male.

'Is there something wrong?' he asked, wiping the moisture from his brow. 'Are you in trouble at Succoth?'

She held out the package he had given her.

'They weren't any use,' she said unsteadily. 'They're almost a carbon copy of my father's from the first expedition. We went over all that ground when he was here last summer.'

'Even though you won't believe me, I'm sorry,' he said, his grey eyes full of sympathy. 'I thought they might have been a help. What are you going to do now?' he asked deliberately.

'We're going away.' She tried not to sound too forlorn. 'My mother has always wanted to live in Barbados, or even in England, where she feels she belongs.'

'And what about you, Makeda?' he asked. 'Where do you belong?'

If she had told the truth she would have cried: 'Here! I belong on this island,' but how could she say such a thing when he now owned Millo and Crichton's was being prepared for his bride?

'I must have a future somewhere,' she said instead, turning her head away to hide the foolish tears which persisted in gathering in her eyes. 'Mother thinks I should train for something more than just a vague typing career.'

'Is that what you want?' he asked. 'A completely new beginning?'

'I suppose I do, since this is the end of something,' she answered. 'Simon believes we're always making choices of one kind or another about our lives. He thinks I could be quite happy in England.'

'Do you?'

He was standing quite close, and suddenly the tremendous magnetism which she had always felt when he was near overwhelmed her.

'I know I have to make my own decisions,' she answered unsteadily, 'but at the moment I'm just—stunned by what's happened. I'll need time to adjust.' It wasn't just the disappointment over the notes she was thinking about. 'Perhaps this is the growing-up process you spoke about, the transition period which you think has been too long delayed in my case. I know it's no use looking back or—or wishing things could be different, and maybe I'll come to terms with it in the end. I hope I will. I don't want to be the sort of person who goes through life saying "If only" this had happened, or that. I haven't any firm plans at present, but Jacinthe means to take up nursing and I may go with her. Abi is already a qualified S.R.N., so we'd be keeping it in the family.' She looked up at him, trying to smile.

'I can't imagine you tending the sick in some crowded city hospital,' he said. 'The Islands are your place, Makeda.'

'Don't keep saying that!' she cried. 'They're the place where I've been happy, but surely there must be happiness for me somewhere else, even though I can't see it just now.'

'You will see it,' he said, taking up the saw. 'I want you to stay at Succoth for as long as you like.'

'How can I do that?' The tears were very near her eyes now. 'I have to go with the others, and there's so little time left.'

He gazed down at the felled tree.

'On Millo,' he reflected slowly, 'there's all the time in the world. Isn't that part of its charm, an island so remote that even time stands still? Don't despair, Makeda. I think your father's notes will turn up and you'll finish his book. For you it was a sacred trust.'

How well he understood. Suddenly, how well he knew what she thought about her father and the task he had begun, the task she had promised herself to finish before she could think of seeking happiness on her own account.

Although she knew that the two were closely linked, the contentment she had known on Millo was a thing of the past. She was restless and unhappy now and one day she would have to go. One day quite soon.

'Mother thinks we should be able to move out by the end of the month,' she said so quickly that the words seemed to tumble out. 'She has friends in Bridgetown where we can stay for a while until we make up our minds about the future. The furniture won't be much of a problem, it's so terribly well worn.'

'Does your mother want to sell it?' he asked almost brutally. 'You know I'm re-furnishing Crichton's.'

'I think she might come to some arrangement with you.' Determinedly Makeda looked straight ahead at the fallen mahogany tree. 'We seem to have stored such a lot of stuff at Succoth over the years, old furniture which my father bought in the Islands and all his books. Mother couldn't possibly take them with her to a modern flat. There just wouldn't be room.'

'Makeda,' he asked quietly, 'would you trust me with his books? I would take good care of them and you could have them back whenever you wished.'

'Oh! Would you?' She could not turn in case the tears of overwhelming gratitude spilled down her cheeks to her eternal shame. 'It would mean so much to know that they were not just stowed away in crates in some stuffy warehouse. Perhaps Simon may want some of them eventually. He's going on with his career.'

Grant allowed the remark about Simon's future to pass into a lengthening silence.

'Let me know what your mother thinks,' he said at last, getting ready to use the saw. 'And in the meantime we'll hope that your father's notes will turn up out of the blue.'

He sounded almost confident that some sort of miracle of recovery would restore them to her, even although he knew now that they would be leaving Millo at the end of the month, of their own free will. They had ended the contract voluntarily, setting him free from the promise George Hunt had made to her father, and no doubt he was greatly relieved.

Walking slowly back to Succoth, Makeda tried not to think of the immediate future, of the days ahead when she would have to say her silent goodbye to everything she loved. There would be no escape from memory, and other memories would pile up to make the inevitable parting doubly hard. She would think of Grant and Crichton's half completed, and Helen waiting to come back to a place in the sun but bound in London by the duties of a wife to a dying husband.

It was almost more than she could bear to look ahead and so she thrust these thoughts firmly into the background of her mind. They would be gone long before Helen's return to Millo, and for that, at least, she should be grateful.

Avoiding a meeting with Simon or any of the others, she took the path on to the beach, easing off her sandals to wade into the clear, green water where it lapped the coral sand. How often she had come here to run and laugh in the sun with Heber and Abi and Jacinthe in the long summer days, or to watch the cormorants and pelicans flying westwards towards the Dutchman's Cap! She had flung herself down on the warm sand in moments of sheer ecstasy, looking up through the palm leaves at the splintered light or listening to the sound of the surf breaking over South Point on a stormy day. It was all her wonderful, secret domain, and even now she could not believe that it was slipping away from her for ever.

Walking on, she climbed to the higher ground beyond the Point where dozens of dolphins came to play in the little, isolated bay which was guarded on both sides by tall cliffs. The Atlantic surf beat endlessly here, seeming to echo her mood as she looked down at the breakers pounding the rocks far beneath her. It was too like the high east coast road at Bathsheba for her to remain there for long, however, and she turned to retrace her steps, realising that she had come a long way in pursuit of her thoughts. It was after one o'clock and Mammy would be fussing and fretting about her absence at the midday meal.

She thought of Mammy and Ben and the children with a great deal of love in her heart. What were they going to do when her mother left for Barbados? On an impulse she had promised to look after them and Mammy had taken her at her word, but it would be no more than a gesture if Dolly refused to help. It was then that she remembered Grant and the need he would have to staff Crichton's. Would he take on Mammy and Ben and six children?

Perhaps she could persuade him that Mammy was an excellent cook and Ben fairly conscientious when there was no urgent work to be done, and the children were so delightful that they were sure to capture his heart. He was not a hard man where children were concerned, as witness his generosity to the fishermen's children when he had been asked to contribute a football pitch and he had cheerfully supplied boots and yellow-and-black striped jerseys into the bargain which had delighted them and made them look like a swarm of very active wasps as they dashed around after the leather ball. Their fathers had worked conscientiously and well at Crichton's and this had been Grant's opportunity to repay them in kind, which had far more value than mere dollars.

When she came within sight of Succoth again she saw Jacinthe approaching the house from the opposite direction. Her cousin had come down from the Bluff by the narrow, winding path, and even from a distance she looked upset. It was plain that she, too, had been absent from the verandah meal. Poor Mammy! Makeda mused with a half-smile. Two truants in one day would be too much for her sense of proportion!

Instead of turning towards the house when she came to the junction of the two paths, Jacinthe came on, meeting Makeda on the beach just short of the jetty where some of the

Crichton stores still lay waiting to be manhandled over the new road.

'What's the matter?' Makeda asked. 'You look like death!'

'I feel like it.' Jacinthe bit her lip. 'You're not going to like this, Makeda, but I've got to tell you.'

'Couldn't it wait till we've reported for lunch?' Makeda asked. 'Once we've put in an appearance on the verandah Mammy will stop having fits and "go make more coffee since this am not fit for the pigs, it am so cold"!'

'Don't joke!' Jacinthe's voice was suddenly hard. 'This is serious—and I'd rather the others didn't hear.'

'By the look of things,' said Makeda, 'there are no "others". Simon and Heber have disappeared and Mother must already be in her room, resting.'

'All the same,' Jacinthe persisted, 'I'd rather tell you out here in the garden.'

'Tell me what?' Makeda asked, puzzled.

Jacinthe drew in a deep breath.

'I stole your father's notes,' she said. 'I took them from the study before Simon started work on them.'

Makeda stared back at her in amazement.

'Why?' she heard herself demanding. 'How could you have done such a thing after all he did for you? We accepted you, Jacinthe, when you had nowhere else to go. You were our cousin and we loved you. We shared our home with you and you were like a sister to us, and now you've done this in return. Why? Why!'

'Because I loved you,' Jacinthe whispered. 'I took the notes to help you, Makeda, because I knew how much Millo meant to you and Heber. I knew Grant would keep his part of the bargain, you see, so if you were never able to finish the book you could stay here always. I did it because I love you,' she repeated. 'Because you've done so much for me.'

Makeda bit back the hasty retort on her lips, silenced by her cousin's tears.

'Where are the notes now?' she asked, an awful suspicion taking shape in her mind. 'You haven't destroyed them?'

Jacinthe shook her head.

'I hid them in the house at first,' she confessed, 'but then, when you and Simon made such a concentrated search for them the other day, I decided to take them on to the Bluff. I went back this morning to see if they were safe and Grant caught me. He said he had a vague idea of what I was doing and he knew *why* I was doing it because he had the same feelings about his uncle, who'd been so kind to him all his life.'

Makeda looked beyond her to the grey rock face beneath the Bluff.

'Did Grant send you to tell me?' she asked.

Her cousin nodded.

'He said it was a very stupid thing to do—a childish reaction, he called it—but he thought it was perfectly understandable and anybody could make a mistake. He had made them himself, he said, although that's difficult to believe. He seems so confident, so assured in his judgment, but that's because he's older and we're really far too young for our age.'

Makeda smiled at her blunt logic.

'Which means we have still time to learn,' she said. 'What have you done with the notes?'

Jacinthe delved into the big, square pocket of her cotton sun-dress.

'They're here,' she said. 'Absolutely intact. I'm sorry I've worried you so much, Makeda. Grant said it was a terrible thing to do.'

'You're forgiven.' Makeda clutched the precious notes. 'I can't wait to tell Simon!'

'Need you?' Jacinthe's voice was shaken. 'I thought—if you could just say that they turned up unexpectedly. You see, he imagined you blamed him in the first place.' The deep colour of painful embarrassment stained her cheeks. 'He would never forgive me if he discovers the truth.'

'When did you fall in love with Simon?' Makeda asked gently.

'I'm not in love with him!'

'Surely you are, otherwise you wouldn't be so concerned.'

'It must have been a long time ago,' Jacinthe said slowly.

'Almost as soon as we met, but he would call it "kitten love" and laugh.'

'I don't think so,' Makeda declared stoutly. 'Simon isn't unkind.'

'Will he stay to help you now that you have the notes back?'

'I don't know. I shall have to ask him,' Makeda decided. 'He was going as far as Bridgetown with you and Mother, and then I think he was flying back to England to look for another job.'

Jacinthe nodded dolefully.

'That's what he planned, but having the notes to be going on with could change everything,' she added optimistically. 'He made himself part of the bargain, didn't he, when Grant agreed to the conditions of his uncle's contract?'

'I could do with his help,' said Makeda, 'although all this might not alter Mother's plans to move out at the end of the month.'

'You and I could stay on,' Jacinthe suggested. 'It wouldn't be the first time we'd been on the island with only Mammy and Ben to look after us.'

'Three weeks should be long enough to finish the book,' Makeda said. 'Then we shall all have to go.'

'It's terribly sad.' Jacinthe led the way along the overgrown path to the house. 'Succoth will miss us.'

'You would have left, anyway, to become a nurse,' Makeda pointed out.

'Which leaves only you, and I know how much you hate the idea of leaving Millo for good,' her cousin said, climbing the rickety steps to the verandah where Mammy was rocking herself to and fro in the old cane rocking-chair in the shade, half asleep and half awake, waiting for them to come in.

Simon came back with Heber for the evening meal.

'I've got the missing notes,' Makeda called to him as he mounted the shallow steps from the garden. 'I've spent all afternoon going through them and they're just what we need.'

' "We"?' he questioned, sitting down beside her. 'Makeda, I can't stay on Millo for ever.'

'But this wouldn't be for ever,' she protested. 'Simon, they found the mine they were looking for—a small one and quite empty—but it had been worked all these years ago.' Her voice rose with excitement. 'Don't you see? It proves everything they believed in and it will be the fitting ending I needed for his book!'

'That's wonderful,' he agreed, some of her enthusiasm reflected in his blue eyes. 'I'll help you while I can, if that's what you really want, but it's high time I got back to civilisation and the daily grind.'

'Simon, you don't mean that!' she cried. 'Why do you want to rush away so soon?'

' "Want" doesn't come into it. I have to go.'

'Simon, why? You meant to stay till the book was finished.'

'Yes,' he agreed, 'but now that everything is practically plain sailing I think you can manage very well without me.'

She felt disappointed, and told him so.

'We worked so well together!'

'And that was all there was to it as far as you were concerned.' He looked into her distressed face. 'I fell in love with you, but I think I must have known from the beginning that I hadn't a ghost of a chance. Now,' he went on relentlessly, 'I can be very noble and say, with a sigh, that at least I have my work. I'll stay with you for another week,' he promised, 'and we'll work like beavers, but after that it's goodbye, Makeda, unless we chance to meet again.'

' "Some other place: some other time"! It seems so far removed from the Islands, Simon, so remote from the life I've lived for so long,' she sighed. 'What will you do when you return to England?'

'Find another job and wait for your book to come out.'

'You'll leave a forwarding address so that I can send you one of the first copies?'

'Of course! I should be terribly disappointed in you if you

164

didn't send me a copy. Think of the prestige it will bring me,' he added lightly. 'My name in print, even if it is only a short acknowledgement of these past few weeks when life has been very kind to me.'

CHAPTER NINE

THEY worked hard for the next few days, sometimes on the verandah when the room at the back of the house became too stuffy for absolute concentration, and sometimes sitting out under the Bluff itself when a cool wind blew in from the sea. There was an unsettled feeling in the air, a breathlessness which could lead to storm, and a brassy-looking sun climbed high over them from Pelican Head to the western horizon each day hidden behind a thin haze which made the heat oppressive.

'We need a good blow to clear all this away,' Heber declared. 'We won't be able to work properly till there's a change in the weather.'

'Is it holding things up at Crichton's?' Makeda asked. 'We haven't seen Grant for almost a week.'

'The men don't work so well in this sort of weather,' Heber allowed. 'It's too exhausting and not what they're used to, but Grant has promised them a Crop Over festival all of their own once Crichton's is finished, so I don't think they'll slack off too much. He's bringing in some furniture by the trader tomorrow, by the way, so he should be able to live in part of the house before long.'

'Has he heard from Helen?' Makeda asked.

'Not yet. He recognises the limitations of living in such a remote place as Millo, and Helen's the sort of person who doesn't write unless she has something important to say.'

Makeda couldn't ask any more questions. She would be far away from Millo before Helen came again to Crichton Place.

The *Fair Trader* came into Frenchman's Cove early the next morning, unloading several large crates with Grant's name on them, but there were no passengers to be put ashore.

Standing at the window of the dining-room, Makeda scanned the deck through binoculars, looking for a flash of blue slacks or the gay challenge of a red bandana, but all she could pick out was the florid countenance of Captain Horatio Bayley and the scurrying figures of his crew.

When the final crate was unloaded on to the jetty Grant came to inspect them. One of them appeared to be a small truck, which was quickly unpacked and loaded for the journey through the scrub to Crichton's. It was all taking shape, Makeda mused. The new road and the restored house, and now Grant had a means of transport which would take him easily about the island wherever he wanted to go. The pick-up, small though it was, would be invaluable to him.

She watched from a distance, thinking how easily he had fitted in and how much he had done to improve her beloved island—for Helen.

The thought remained an ache in her heart as she worked with Simon on the final part of her father's book. With luck, she would finish it and have it on its way to New York by the end of the month.

Mammy appeared in the study doorway with the mail from the trader. There were several letters for her mother and one from the London solicitor's office forwarded from Bridgetown by Gothram, Tyndall and Pettigrew. Helen hadn't written, although she had promised to do so.

'Mr Ogilvie he say he want a word with yo', Mr Wetherby,' Mammy announced. 'He waitin' outside in de porch.'

Makeda's heart lurched.

'Coming?' Simon asked, looking across at her.

She shook her head.

'I'll see what Mr Pettigrew has sent,' she decided, opening the manilla envelope which Mammy had handed to her.

When Simon returned he said abruptly:

'Time's up, Makeda. I'm going out with *Seafarer* the day after tomorrow. Grant is going over to Grenada to pick up some more cargo and he's offered me a berth.'

'It's all too sudden!' Makeda's eyes were stormy. 'Everything is coming to an end so terribly quickly. Another week and the MS too will be on its way to Grenada to catch the mail plane for New York.'

'It's been a wonderful achievement on your part,' he said. 'A sort of fulfilment when it was the one thing you wanted to do.'

Perhaps the sense of fulfilment should have cancelled out the terrible feeling of loss she now felt, but she knew that her heart was almost breaking as she wondered about the future. Two more days and Simon would be gone, and after that it would be her own turn to say goodbye to all she loved and would ever hold dear.

Two days later Grant brought *Seafarer* round to the Cove to pick up Simon and his luggage. The ketch came right in to the end of the jetty and Makeda walked down with Simon to say goodbye. It had all happened so quickly in the end; Simon leaving and her Mother with most of her plans for the future already made, and Grant, too, had his plans for Millo in which she had no part.

Dolly took a rather sentimental farewell of their guest, while Jacinthe looked on with a bleak sort of acceptance of the inevitability of parting never to meet again.

Simon turned to her almost as an afterthought.

'If you ever come to London,' he said, 'you must look me up. I have a small pad in Pimlico, overlooking the river, where I can be contacted most of the time. I've left the address with your aunt.'

Jacinthe said eagerly, her eyes glowing with anticipation:

'I'd like that. I've decided to go in for nursing and I hope to train at a London hospital.' She glanced back to where Dolly stood at the end of the jetty. 'It doesn't really depend on Aunt Dolly. I'd be staying in the hostel, like Abi did.'

Simon turned his attention to Makeda.

'Goodbye, my love,' he said gently. 'I've very little hope that you'll change your mind, but if you do I'll be waiting.'

It was the dramatic response to the situation that Makeda might have expected of him, but she could not put it into perspective with a light word of dismissal.

'You'll meet someone else,' she said quietly, hoping that it would be Jacinthe. 'London must be full of lovely girls.'

'Full to overflowing,' he admitted, walking with her a little way along the jetty, 'but the answer to that one is that they're not like you.'

Grant was standing beside the ketch, waiting. He had carried Simon's luggage aboard and now he seemed impatient to set sail. Deliberately Simon took her into his arms.

'"Ae fond kiss",' he quoted, his blue eyes denying the lightness of his tone. 'If you ever come to London, etc., etc! I'll miss you, Makeda,' he added. 'I'll miss our work together, and Millo and the Islands, but I have to go.'

He bent his head to kiss her full on the lips, a long, lingering kiss which he knew in his heart was a last farewell, and Makeda stood on the jetty where he left her watching as Grant strode across *Seafarer*'s deck to unfurl the mainsail. He raised a hand in brief salute when Simon was aboard and then the gangplank went up and they had sailed away.

A brisk little wind took them swiftly out of the Cove, but it died before the afternoon was over. Makeda worked on the final chapter of the book till three o'clock, when it became too hot to concentrate properly. Dolly had gone to lie down and Jacinthe had followed Heber to Crichton's where she had promised Grant to unpack some curtain material which he had brought over on his last trip to Grenada. It would have been Helen's job if she had been there, Makeda thought, wandering restlessly beneath the coconut palms.

The overpowering atmosphere lasted for another two days. 'It'll end in a terrific blow,' Heber predicted. 'It always does, although I've never known it take so long to break.'

Hurricane Nessie was announced over the radio the following morning. Heber had gone across to Crichton's earlier than usual and Jacinthe had probably followed him because she was nowhere to be seen when Makeda went out on to the verandah after her morning swim. The water in the Cove had been still and green and positively warm, and she had stood under her shower afterwards, wishing that the storm would break. There was no real danger to Millo since the trajectory of the hurricane was north-west of their position, but hurricanes were unpredictable things at the best of times, and she went in search of Ben.

'We'll have to do what we can about the roof, just in case,' she told him. 'If there are any tiles that might come adrift see what you can do about battening them down. Any makeshift thing will do.'

'Am de ol' blow comin' straight for us, Miss Makeda?' he asked in a matter-of-fact tone which made her smile. 'Maybe it blow some other way.'

'If it keeps on its present track it will miss us altogether, but there's bound to be a lot of wind,' Makeda reminded him. 'After you've fixed the roof see what you can do about your own home, Ben, and keep the children clear of the trees when it does come.'

Ben went off to do her bidding, and she returned to the house to comfort Dolly, who had been informed about the coming hurricane by Mammy as soon as she had appeared on the verandah.

'I can't do with this kind of heat,' Dolly complained. 'It leaves me like a limp rag. Do you realise that it's ninety-odd in the shade? And then this "blow", as Mammy calls it! I've only seen one hurricane in all the years I've been coming here, and that was terrifying. What can we possibly do?'

'Sit it out,' Makeda said with as much conviction as she could command. 'We might only get the edge of it here.'

'The *edge*?' Dolly repeated fearfully. 'What does that mean?'

'The worst will pass us by. I'm not pretending there won't be a lot of wind or even some damage, but we're nowhere near the centre of the disturbance.'

'I wish we'd gone off with Simon and left Succoth to its fate!' Dolly declared.

'Mother, don't panic! We'll survive all right if we take the necessary precautions,' Makeda pointed out. 'Nobody is likely to do anything foolish when there's a blow around. Anyway, we've got Heber, who's a tower of strength in an emergency.'

'Heber isn't at Succoth,' Dolly complained. 'I expect he's over at Crichton Place making sure that the new roof stays on!' She took a couple of paces about the verandah. 'Where was Jacinthe going?' she demanded.

'To Crichton's, I expect. Grant asked her to look at some curtains.'

'She could easily have walked across,' Dolly said testily. 'What made her take the dinghy?'

'The dinghy?' Makeda rose quickly to her feet. 'How do you know?'

'I saw her. She went off just after you came in.'

'The dinghy was at the jetty while I was down on the beach.' Makeda was hardly speaking to the anxious woman sitting at the table in her flowered dressing-gown. She was calculating the sequence of events which had led to her cousin going off alone in a sailing dinghy with the possibility of a hurricane hitting them within the hour. 'It was almost too hot to swim, so I came back to have a shower. Why did she do it? She must have heard the warning.'

'I didn't,' Dolly pointed out. 'Mammy told me when she brought my tea. These islands are fraught with danger,' she rushed on, 'and people talk about Paradise!'

Makeda wasn't listening.

'What way did Jacinthe go?' She was already half-way down the verandah steps. 'Did you see?'

'She seemed to be making for the Dutchman's Cap.'

'She wouldn't get half-way there,' Makeda frowned. 'She doesn't know enough about handling a boat on her own. Surely she would have the sense to keep along the coast, and even then it would be a foolhardy adventure if she knew about the blow.'

'She looked upset,' Dolly remembered, coming to the verandah rail. 'Don't you remember how she used to go off on her own when she was in a mood?'

'I don't think this was a "mood" as you mean it,' Makeda said over her shoulder. 'I think she was deeply distressed.'

'Oh, my goodness!' said Dolly. 'We can't all go rushing off at a tangent because we've been left behind. If she really does care for Simon she'll meet him again in London. I have his address.'

Her voice carried over the hush of the garden as Makeda took the path to the Bluff. It was very still now, with not even a breath of wind to stir the palms, and the sun was hidden behind a brazen layer of cloud which seemed to press the heat down on to the rocks and the glassy cove. When she reached the highest point of the Bluff she left the path, scrambling along the edge of the cliff to scan the sea, but although the Dutchman's Cap stood out clearly enough on the western horizon there was no sign of a sail anywhere. It was a red sail she was looking for, something easy to pick out on that vast expanse of grey-blue ocean lying under the pall of the oppressive heat, but the whole world seemed to be empty. There was not even a single fishing boat making its way round South Point to the safety of Morgan's Reach before the storm broke.

Green Turtle! she thought, but if Jacinthe had gone there it was a foolish gesture to make. To an experienced sailor the reef was the most treacherous obstacle on the entire coastline, and her cousin was far from experienced.

Her heart pounding, she ran back to the path, wondering what to do when she finally reached the bay. Grant had gone out on *Seafarer* and there was no other boat available as far as she knew. Heber might be there, however, or some of the native workers who had been busy at Crichton's.

She came at last to the edge of the escarpment where she could look down into Green Turtle Bay, and her heart lurched when she saw the longboat pulled up on the sand. It was new and glossy and the very thing she might need if there was any sign of Jacinthe beyond the reef.

Scanning the bay, she could make out the thin white line which marked the coral and the knife-edge end to the reef. There was only the narrowest of channels between it and the treacherous rocks of the Albatross Bank, but to anyone who knew it, as she did, it was passable.

Passable in a reasonably calm sea, she reminded herself. Jacinthe had sailed with her many times through the gap into Green Turtle Bay, but it had always been Makeda's hand on the tiller and her firm grip on the sheets.

Beyond the reef the sea looked flat and oily with the outline of Pelican Island no more than a thin blur on the horizon, and then, out of nowhere, a little wind began to blow. At first it was no more than a whisper, but within minutes it rose to a whine. It increased as it swept in across the coral and over the bay to the sandy shore and soon it engulfed the whole island. Slender trees bowed before it, but the great mahoganies faced it with little more than a tremor of their leaves.

When she turned again to the sea Makeda saw a flash of red against the distant island and knew that it was a sail. Somewhere out there beyond the reef Jacinthe was struggling with the rising wind as she made a desperate effort to reach the bay.

Looking up at Crichton's it seemed to be completely deserted and Makeda supposed that Heber and most of the workmen had gone to Morgan's Reach to help the villagers batten down everything before the hurricane actually struck. She had seconds to make up her mind what to do. The volume of the wind was steadily increasing and precious time would be lost if she climbed up to Crichton's to ask for help.

Once, and then again, she shouted, but there was no reply and the red sail was coming perilously near the reef. She pushed the longboat down the beach, scarcely stopping to think that it was no task for someone on their own, and once in the water she pulled at the heavy oars with amazing strength. The wind was now gale force and the reef was a mile away.

She could still see the dinghy battling with the sea, it's red sail flung from side to side as Jacinthe attempted to reach the narrow gap between the coral and the rock. If she hit the Albatross Bank she would be in real danger, but Makeda's intention was to go through the gap and reach her while she was still outside the reef.

The rising wind tossed her calculations aside. It came in from the direction of Pelican Island, screaming over the reef and the bay until she knew that the full force of the storm would soon be upon her. Hurricane Nessie had changed course, like a capricious woman, and was tearing her way towards Millo at an incredible speed.

The dinghy hit the reef before she reached it and she saw Jacinthe clinging to the gunwale with the broken mast and torn sail tossing on the sea.

'I'm coming!' she shouted. 'Hold on!' But the wind snatched her words away, carrying them towards the treacherous Albatross Bank which seemed to be coming nearer and nearer as she pulled madly at the oars.

All the strength she could muster was put into the next few minutes. Jacinthe was a strong swimmer and she would have to play her part in her own rescue. When she saw the long-boat she turned on her back, still clasping the gunwale.

'Swim!' Makeda shouted. 'Swim for your life!'

'I—can't!' Jacinthe's faint response came over the whine of the wind. 'I can't make it——'

'You must!' With renewed strength Makeda pulled the last few yards between the two boats. 'You've got to swim,' she yelled. 'I can't come any nearer. Don't argue, Jacinthe—just swim!'

Her heart raced as she watched her cousin make the supreme effort, but she could do nothing further to help. It was almost more than she could manage to keep the prow of her own craft head on to the wind, and when Jacinthe finally tumbled into the longboat she knew that she could not have sustained the effort much longer.

Jacinthe began to cry.

'Oh, Makeda, I've wrecked your dinghy,' she sobbed. 'I didn't mean to come so far. I'm sorry! I'm sorry!'

'Sit and grab the other pair of oars,' said Makeda. 'We'll both have to pull like mad to get back into the bay.'

'What is it?' Jacinthe asked, gripping the heavy oars. 'A hurricane?'

Makeda nodded.

'We're in it, right up to our necks,' she said through clenched teeth. 'Didn't you hear the radio warning?'

Jacinthe shook her head.

'I went out before eight o'clock.' She gazed fearfully towards the churning sea where it boiled along the reef. 'Are we going to drown?'

'Maybe,' said Makeda, 'but if we are we're going to drown rowing this boat! We're not going to make the gap, and even if we did there's no guarantee we'd get through in this sea. We've got to try for Pelican Island, otherwise we'll be thrown on to the Albatross. In this sea it will be covered in no time.'

It was the last conversation they had before they were tossed like a piece of flotsam on to Pelican Island. A single great wave, the first of many, had caught them, lifting them like a detached palm-leaf on to the rocky shore.

Makeda gripped her cousin's hand.

'Jump when the next wave lifts us,' she commanded. 'If it fills the boat we're done for.'

They jumped simultaneously, climbing high on to the deserted island as the following wave swamped their borrowed craft.

'We could have gone down with it!' Jacinthe gasped. 'And we're not out of danger, are we? If we do get the full force of the hurricane we won't have an earthly chance out here. The waves will be enormous——'

'Stop it!' Makeda cried. 'We'll have to think of something else to do.'

In spite of her effort to reassure her frightened companion, there was fear in her own heart. Ever since her childhood she had been warned about Pelican Island and the Albatross Bank and she had always given them a wide berth, but here she was sitting on the island without any means of returning to Green Turtle Bay and with the vanguard wind of a hurricane blowing hotly against her cheek.

The molten orb of the sun disappeared behind a thicker layer of cloud, bringing a strange chill to the atmosphere, and everything seemed to be standing still again, waiting. In the ensuing silence Jacinthe looked across at her with anxious eyes.

'Are we going to die?' she asked. 'I've read about people being trapped like this and all their past came rushing back to them. I haven't much past,' she added shakily. 'Neither have you, Makeda. Were you in love with Simon?'

Makeda shook her head.

'Never. We worked well together, that was all, and I don't feel as if my whole past should be rushing towards me!' She emphasised the fact with a shaky laugh. 'We ought to be thinking of ways and means to survive, somewhere deep enough for us to dig in.' She looked about her at the shelving rocks. 'If we're lucky the wind might go over us.'

'Even in an ordinary storm most of the island is submerged,' Jacinthe reminded her, 'and this isn't an ordinary storm.'

'We'll try, anyway.' Makeda scrambled to her feet. 'Follow me as closely as you can.'

The wind, waiting in the wings, began to murmur its disapproval as they climbed to the highest part of the island and neither of them heard the other boat coming up behind them. When they did the strong beat of the powerful engine was unbelievable, at first, like a mirage in the desert, but *Seafarer* had passed on into the anchorage at Green Turtle Bay before they could attempt any kind of distress signal.

They could stand on the island and wave, Makeda thought desperately, but it would all be to no avail, yet the fact that Grant had returned to Green Turtle Bay drove some of the fear from her heart.

'Surely they'll search for us,' Jacinthe said. 'They must know we're missing by now.'

It was almost an hour before they heard the sound of the engine again and by that time the murmur of the angry wind had risen to a howl. It flayed the sea, tearing at the island as it rushed towards Millo, but they knew that this was only the forerunner of worse to come. It was impossible to see the approaching boat for the curtain of spume which rose before the wind, but the strong beat of the powerful engine gave them hope.

Jacinthe stood on the highest rock she could find waving

frantically, although she was almost blown off her feet doing so.

'It's no good,' she said at last, sinking down beside Makeda. 'They'll pass us by. They couldn't possibly see us through all this spume.'

Almost while she was speaking the engine cut out. It was an impossible landing on the windward side of the island and just about as impossible on the lee side, but Makeda pulled her cousin with her as she clambered over the top and slid down the steep sand-dunes towards the sea where they could look across the treacherous Albatross Bank to Millo.

They saw Grant then, coming towards them in *Seafarer*'s dinghy, but for a moment neither of them could believe that he was really there. Jacinthe was first to let out a long-drawn breath.

'We're saved!' she cried hysterically. 'We're really saved. It's Grant!'

Makeda could see the difficulty he was in, doing his best to keep the dinghy afloat. He had throttled back the outboard engine to come close inshore, but the sea was lifting the dinghy at a crazy angle, slapping it down again as if it would tear out its hull with one savage blow. Grant would never make it, she thought, while she prayed in her heart that he would.

Presently dinghy and man disappeared completely behind an enormous roller which the rising wind had whipped from behind the reef and flung at them in an excess of violence, and in the ensuing pause she realised that the outboard had been silenced.

Still running, they reached the lee shore where, miraculously, the wind had subsided for a moment to draw breath for the next onslaught. Grant was there, drawing the dinghy up the shelving beach.

'What in heaven's name made you go out with a blow coming on?' he greeted them angrily as they rushed towards him.

His face was so tense that Makeda hardly recognised him;

tense with rage, she supposed, and contempt for her lack of judgment.

'It wasn't Makeda's fault! You mustn't blame her.' Jacinthe rushed in with the truth before Makeda could answer him. 'She came in search of me when she heard the warning. I brought the sailing dinghy round from Frenchman's, but I hadn't heard the radio warning and it was too late to turn back when I realised what was happening. I—lost the dinghy on the reef.' She covered her face with her hands, shivering as the full force of her 'adventure' came home to her. 'It was horrible. Horrible!' she repeated.

Grant straightened, his mouth still hard with disapproval, but some of the harshness gone from his eyes.

'Are you all right?' he asked.

'As right as—as we can be.'

Makeda's heart was pounding against her ribs, not only from the latent effects of fear but because Grant was standing there beside her, so near that she could have flung herself into his arms just by taking one small step across the sand-dunes. It was irrational to feel that all was now well because they were still in grave danger, but the fact of his presence dispelled fear. If there was anything to be done Grant would do it, even in the path of a hurricane. The strength of the man gave her fresh courage and a little hope.

He looked down to where the dinghy lay, then up at the sky, taking a full minute to assess the situation.

'We're not going to make it across to Millo,' he said briskly. 'We'd never survive out there. We'll have to dig ourselves in. That way, we can take a chance of it going right over us.' He glanced at his watch. 'We've got about fifteen minutes and then all hell will break loose. There's no time to waste.'

They dug with their bare hands, hauling up a spar of driftwood to act as a batten against the possibility of the makeshift cave falling in on them, by which time the wind had risen to a scream and the terrible sound of a hurricane was fully upon them.

Grant pushed Jacinthe into the shelter.

'Lie down,' he commanded. 'As flat as you can.'

Makeda stood beside him while Jacinthe did his bidding, curling herself into the back of the improvised cave to make room for them to follow her.

'Now, Makeda,' he said.

She hesitated for a moment, looking into his eyes, trying to speak.

'Get in!' he ordered sharply. 'There's a time and place for argument.'

'Grant,' she said when he had squeezed in beside her, blocking the narrow entrance to their hideaway with the sheer bulk of his powerful body, 'I wasn't going to argue. I was—trying to thank you.'

'Some other time,' he suggested brusquely, putting a protective arm about her. 'With any kind of luck we should see this through.'

His nearness was warmth and comfort and sudden recompense for all the turmoil of the past few weeks, and she lay there beside him, content to wait.

Then, as if some inferno of wave and wind had suddenly broken above them, the hurricane found Pelican Island and Green Turtle Bay, screaming its way across the reef into the anchorage and over the Bluff to tear the scrub out by the roots and snap off the coconut palms half way up their trunks. Even from where they cowered on the lee side of Pelican they could hear the dreadful sound of falling trees and waves tearing their way towards the shore.

'Millo?' Makeda whispered. 'Everything will be gone—devastated by this terrible wind. And Succoth——'

Grant drew her close against him.

'Don't think about it,' he advised. 'It's something we can't do much about, but if it's any comfort to you, Heber must be at Succoth by now. He was on his way there when I went into the anchorage with *Seafarer*.'

'Will she be safe?' Makeda asked, her head against the warm comfort of his shoulder.

'She's anchored close in to the reef. I think she may survive.'

The snarl of the wind grew to an awful howl, rising in a sheer crescendo to a fiendish banshee wail which lasted for several minutes, subsiding briefly until it repeated itself with what seemed to be renewed fury. It would go on and on for ever, Makeda thought, growing in intensity until it tore the whole island apart.

It blew for twenty minutes, shifting part of the Albatross Bank as it passed, but their shelter remained intact. Then the dreadful sound of the raging wind seemed to recede into the distance and Grant moved his cramped position and took his arm away from her shoulders.

'That's about it,' he said in the most matter-of-fact tone she had ever heard. 'We can be back on Millo in half an hour.'

The rain came in a silence which could almost be felt, pouring down in a sheet of water through which it was difficult to see, and Makeda knew that Grant was far more anxious about their makeshift shelter now than he had been even at the height of the storm.

'We're going to get very wet,' he said, 'but we must get away from here. Are you all right, Jacinthe?' he asked when there was no immediate response from the rear of the 'cave'.

Jacinthe's teeth were chattering. Reaction had set in and it was several minutes before she could speak.

'This was all my fault,' she said bleakly. 'I deserved to die.'

'Don't be foolish!' Grant was speaking as he would have spoken to Makeda several weeks ago. 'You can't hold yourself responsible for a hurricane any more than I can.'

'I should never have taken the dinghy in the first place,' Jacinthe sobbed, 'but I wanted to get away and it seemed quite safe to come as far as Green Turtle on my own.'

It was a sad little expression of youthful, blighted love and Grant took it seriously enough.

'Nobody will blame you, Jacinthe,' he said. 'We all have to rush away from ourselves at times.'

'There's something else,' Makeda confessed, shifting her cramped position beside him. 'Your new longboat. I took it to row out to the reef when I saw the dinghy in trouble. It must be gone now, Grant. We had no hope of saving it. I'm sorry.'

'What's a boat among friends?' He looked down at her with frank amusement in his grey eyes now that the tension had passed. 'We're lucky enough in that respect,' he added. 'I insured her yesterday before I left Bridgetown!'

He was putting things on a practical level mainly to re-assure Jacinthe, but Makeda knew that something had changed between them. The past two hours had cemented a friendship and respect which could never be eroded, and that was all she could hope for. She had grown up in Grant's estimation; the child had flown away in the wake of the hurricane.

When the rain finally eased a little they emerged from their temporary shelter to survey the damage. Part of the Bank had shifted, but *Seafarer*'s tender lay untouched on the shore.

'We've been amazingly lucky,' Grant said, helping them to their feet. 'I must confess I was worried about our hide-away. Now for Millo!'

It was impossible to see the other island for the driving rain and Jacinthe said fearfully:

'Do you think it's still there?'

Grant laughed with an easing of tension which they could all feel.

'Islands don't just blow away,' he declared. 'The Bluff will have sheltered Frenchman's, and I've no real fear for Crichton's.'

Jacinthe made a tremendous effort to pull herself together.

'If your engine won't start, Grant, we can all row,' she offered. 'I'm really quite good at it.'

'I'm sure you are!' He put a comforting arm about her. 'I accept your offer unreservedly!'

He did not look at Makeda as they walked down the shelv-ing dune towards the small, inadequate tender which had brought him across Green Turtle Bay to their rescue.

'Do you think Succoth will be all right?' Jacinthe asked.

'We can keep our fingers crossed,' he decided.

He was not so sure about Succoth, Makeda realised as the nagging little fear in her own heart increased. Succoth was partly sheltered by the Bluff, but Hurricane Nessie had ploughed her way towards them from the south-west and the Cove was open to that direction.

'Heber will have seen to everything,' Grant tried to assure her. 'Don't worry too much.'

'Can you imagine my mother in a situation like this?' she asked. 'She'll be terrified, and Mammy won't be much help. She's superstitious about blows. She believes that all the fiends there are come in a big wind to devastate the land. The amazing thing is that Ben will be the real tower of strength in all this. He realises that hurricanes are natural phenomena and he knows how to deal with them. I've never known Ben to go to pieces in an emergency.'

Grant was trying to start the outboard. It resisted his first few attempts, sputtering out to a tense silence while he tried again. The rain had eased and visibility had become a little clearer as the head of the Bluff appeared and the long chain of the reef, bathed in a sudden shaft of sunlight. It was like a promise.

Far to the west a flock of cormorants rose, making their way south, and suddenly the whole of Millo was there for them to see. Grant's gaze went straight to Crichton Place which stood as he had left it above the shore. Otherwise, the damage was obvious, whichever way they looked. Hurricane Nessie had torn a path across Millo which had devastated a great part of the island. Palm trees lay at crazy angles, their tops lopped off as if a giant with an axe had passed among them, hacking as he went, and vast patches of scrub had been torn out by the roots. Only the magnificent avenue of mahogany trees which marked the way to Crichton's remained and a few of the more sheltered groves of palm along the shore.

They piled into the tender as the outboard sputtered into life, and almost in no time they were inside the reef and speeding towards the shore. *Seafarer* lay close to the reef where Grant had anchored when he had first come in. She was untouched.

Heber came to meet them down the sloping path to the beach.

'He seems to be in one piece,' Grant observed with a note of relief in his voice. 'I hope everyone else is safe.'

Inwardly Makeda echoed his words. Her whole family had been there, at Succoth, with the exception of Abi. What had happened to them?

Grant ran the tender in over the shallow water, shut off the outboard and jacked it up as the keel sank into the sand. In the silence they could have heard an indrawn breath.

'Thank heaven you're safe!' Heber cried as he waded into the water to help them ashore. 'I knew you would find them, if anyone could,' he added to Grant. 'It's been quite a blow!'

'The others?' Makeda asked. 'Mother and Mammy and Ben and the children?'

'Ben has been exceptional,' Heber acknowledged. 'When the roof went he had everything organised. Mother, of course, had several near-fits, but she pulled herself together when she saw how Ben was coping and it was only the roof that had gone. She's declaring, of course, that she'll never set foot in Succoth again. This has been a warning!'

He was endeavouring to make light of their plight at Succoth, but the fact that her old home had been so badly damaged forced the tears to Makeda's eyes.

'This must be the end,' she said, 'but we were lucky we all survived.'

'I took the others to Crichton's,' Heber said to Grant as they walked in procession towards the house. 'The damage has been mostly on this side of the island. Everything seems to be O.K. at Morgan's Reach, including the fishing boats. They took a slight battering, but the village didn't suffer much. A few roofs missing and that sort of thing. The camp is still in one piece, thank goodness, so we have plenty of eager hands to repair what damage there is.'

Grant turned to Makeda.

'Don't worry too much about Succoth,' he said, as if he had read her thoughts. 'We'll soon put things straight, and meanwhile you'll stay at Crichton's with your family.'

How could she refuse his offer of shelter when there was absolutely no other alternative? And did she want to refuse? In spite of the fact that he had prepared Crichton Place for someone else she felt that she was coming home.

She looked up at the house with its magnificent colonnaded portico and down on the scene of devastation on the shore; seeing the broken coconut palms and the torn scrub as something she would remember for a very long time, yet the shattered coastline would soon renew itself and Green Turtle would be the same as it had always been. The scars would disappear and the bay would smile again, lying tranquilly inside the reef as if this terrible storm had never been.

Grant took her arm to help her up the steepest part of the incline and, ahead of them, she saw the magnificent avenue of mahogany trees standing, tall and unscathed, on either side of the way.

The way to Crichton's! Her heart seemed to miss a beat as she walked on with Grant by her side, thinking how wonderful it would be if this was their true homecoming.

The great mahogany door lay open, exposing the ancient hall to view with its new rafters and a huge wood fire burning in the massive fireplace at its farthest end. There was very little furniture as yet—an ancient refectory table made from some dark wood which had always been there, and several chairs, all high-backed and uncomfortable which Grant had used, off and on, when he slept at Crichton's overnight. The stone floor remained uncovered, but it had been cleaned and sanded, ready for Helen to spread her Persian rugs in the right places.

'Makeda! Thank God you're safe! And Jacinthe!' On a less enthusiastic note Dolly embraced her niece. 'I don't know why you had to go off as you did, complicating everything. The hurricane was bad enough!'

Almost in tears again, Jacinthe expressed her sorrow as her aunt subsided into the nearest chair.

'I have a splitting headache,' she mourned, 'and Mammy doesn't seem to be able to do anything about it.'

'Get her to bed,' Grant advised. 'You can use my room. There isn't much in it, but at least I treated myself to a decent mattress. Later on we'll salvage what we can from Succoth.' He walked towards the staircase, helping Dolly up the first few stairs. 'A good sleep will work wonders,' he added generously. 'Don't start thinking about the future till you've given it a good try.'

Makeda attempted to pass him with a brief smile of gratitude, but he detained her with a firm hand on her arm.

'Get out of these wet clothes,' he advised. 'You'll find a dressing-gown on the back of the bedroom door. I don't want to see you standing around dripping water all over the place when I come up with some hot punch for your mother. Jacinthe is small enough to make do with a bath towel,' he added with a grin.

'Grant, I——'

'Don't argue the point. I'm giving you ten minutes till the water boils for the punch!' he said.

Mammy, cured of her tears, bustled up to help Dolly into bed.

'Yo' fair worn out, Miss Garland!' she declared, although probably Dolly had done nothing but complain. 'Yo' jus' lie down there an' rest yo'self like Mister Ogilvie say an' tomorrow yo' be good an' well an' you can go back to Succoth.'

'Never!' Dolly exclaimed. 'Ben will pack my things and I'll catch the next trader to Barbados. If Heber wishes to stay, he can, but Makeda and Jacinthe will come with me.'

Mammy's face fell and her great bosom heaved with emotion, but she would not ask what was to become of her. Makeda took Grant's dressing-gown from the hook behind the bedroom door. It was old and worn and smelt of pipe tobacco and it had lost its cord, but it was also a huge and warm comfort to wrap herself in now that the final decision about leaving Millo had been made.

Of course she would go with her mother; of course she would stay in Bridgetown till all Dolly's plans were made and she was happily settled in a new home, but for today, for these few precious hours, she was here at Crichton's and she would savour the bitter-sweet joy of being secure under Grant's roof without a thought for the future.

Peeling off her wet clothes in the adjacent bathroom, she towelled herself vigorously before she wrapped the dressing-gown around her, turning up the sleeves to regain the use of her hands and using her own belt to hoist the trailing ends off the floor.

'You look like a bedraggled mandarin!' Jacinthe laughed, coming in to find another towel. 'Grant must have bought it in China a hundred years ago!' She fingered the embroidered silk of the dressing-gown. 'I expect it's warm enough, though, and a hot punch will complete the cure. I've been sneezing, so Aunt Dolly thinks we're all going to catch pneumonia.'

'I hope not,' Makeda said. 'How many beds are there?'

'Two, I think. The one your mother is using and a second one in another bedroom along the corridor. Helen was doing the curtains in there before she left.'

Grant appeared at the open door with a tray in his hands. There were three mugs of steaming rum punch on it and Mammy handed them round.

'Drink up,' he said, waiting for the empty mugs.

When Makeda finally put them back on the tray he held the bedroom door open.

'Jacinthe can stay with your mother,' he said. 'There's something I want you to see.'

Makeda followed him from the room. Her hair was still wet, but the rum punch had sent a warm glow through her and she had wrapped the dressing-gown more closely around her with a new awareness of her slim, naked body underneath. Helen seemed to be receding into the background with every step they took.

Finally, at the far end of the corridor, Grant flung open a heavily-carved door to reveal a fully-furnished bedroom beyond it. Without speaking he walked towards the two long windows leading out on to a balcony, waiting for

Makeda to follow him, and then he stood aside so that she could look out.

'What do you think of it?' he asked.

Beyond the stone balustrade of the balcony the whole island lay spread out before them, from Morgan's Reach in the north to Dolphins in the east and the smooth top of South Point in the distance. She could even see the head of the Cove and the shattered rooftop of Succoth under the palms which had miraculously survived the storm.

'It must have been the view David Crichton saw when he first planned the house,' she said. 'He must have looked out from this hill and said: "I want to spend my life here and live on this island till I die!"' She turned to look at the new owner of Crichton's, her eyes enormous in the returning light. 'I'm sure that was how it was, Grant. Perfectly sure!'

In one swift, decisive movement he had taken her into his arms.

'Is that how it's going to be for me?' he demanded. 'You're the rest of my life, Makeda. It's for you to say. I started to rebuild Crichton's because I wanted a place of my own, but now I know it will never be complete unless you stay here, unless we finish it together.' He held her at arms' length, searching her face for the truth. 'Tell me you'll stay at Crichton's, where you belong.'

'Oh, Grant!' She hid her face in her hands. 'What kind of a dream is this?'

'No dream!' He pulled her hands away, bending to kiss her on the lips. 'Dreams are poor things when you can walk with reality. We can make Millo the sort of place we've both dreamed about, but the reality will be our love. We can finish Crichton's together and restore Succoth, and Mammy can look after it for Heber or anyone else who wants to come. We may have to range the world in pursuit of a living, but there will always be this island which brought us together in the first place.'

She slipped her arms about his waist and he crushed her to him until she could feel the tautness of his body against her own.

'One day, you said, I would have to grow up,' she whispered.

'And have you?' He smiled down into her happy eyes.

'You know I have! I love you, Grant. I'll always love you.'

'What more could you say?' He turned her round to look again on Millo from their high vantage-point and she saw it lying now in strong sunlight. 'There it is, Sheba,' he said, using the old name with which he had teased her so often. 'Our island!'

Send for free catalog

Most of these old favorites have not been reissued since first publication. So if you read them then, you'll enjoy them again; if they're new to you, you'll have the pleasure of discovering a new series of compelling romances from past years.

Collection Editions are available only from Harlequin Reader Service. They are not sold in stores.

Clip and mail this special coupon. We will send you a catalog listing all the Collection Editions titles and authors.

Harlequin Presents...

By popular demand...
24 original novels from this series—by 7 of the world's greatest romance authors.

These back issues have been out of print for some time. So don't miss out; order your copies now!

Harlequin Reader Service
ORDER FORM

Mail coupon to:
Harlequin Reader Service
M.P.O Box 707
Niagara Falls, New York 14302

Canadian Residents send to:
649 Ontario St.
Stratford, Ont. N5A 6W2

Please send me by return mail the Harlequin Presents that I have checked.

I am enclosing $1.25 for each book ordered.

Please check volumes requested:

☐ 38	☐ 46	☐ 54
☐ 39	☐ 47	☐ 55
☐ 40	☐ 48	☐ 56
☐ 41	☐ 49	☐ 57
☐ 42	☐ 50	☐ 58
☐ 43	☐ 51	☐ 59
☐ 44	☐ 52	☐ 60
☐ 45	☐ 53	☐ 61

Number of books ordered _____ @ $1.25 each = $ _____

N.Y. and N.J. residents add appropriate sales tax $ _____

Postage and handling = $ _____ .25

TOTAL = $ _____

NAME _____
(please print)

ADDRESS _____

CITY _____

STATE/PROV. _____ ZIP/POSTAL CODE _____

ROM 2142